Christmas 1978
From: Aunt Nancy
I'd Love Aunt Nancy

THE BOBBSEY TWINS
AND THE
DOODLEBUG MYSTERY

A doodlebug's a bug
Except when he is not!
Oh, the things a doodlebug can be!
There are a lot!

One doodlebug's a person
Who does a magic trick—
Finds water underground
With a hazel stick!

At a hotel in the mountains the Bobbsey twins meet a very grumpy old doodlebug. He accuses Robin Talltree, the pretty young Indian girl, of stealing his bird-watching equipment from an ancient stone tower across the lake.

"She couldn't have!" says Nan. "She's too nice!"

When the Bobbseys try to find the real thief, things really start popping. Thrills mount as the twins learn the secret of the dancing sticks, catch the tower "spooks," and make their new friends happy, including even grumpy Mr. Doodlebug.

THE BOBBSEY TWINS
By Laura Lee Hope

"Someone's throwing stones at us!" Nan cried

The Bobbsey Twins and the Doodlebug Mystery

By

LAURA LEE HOPE

GROSSET & DUNLAP
Publishers   New York

PRINTED IN THE UNITED STATES OF AMERICA
LIBRARY OF CONGRESS CATALOG CARD NO. 69-16138
ISBN: 0-448-08062-1
The Bobbsey Twins and the Doodlebug Mystery

CONTENTS

CHAPTER I

FLYING CARPET

"HERE comes the doodlebug and he's mad enough to bite!" cried a young man as he dashed past the Bobbsey twins.

He had run from the porch into the lobby of the Sky House, a summer hotel.

"What's a doodlebug?" Bert and Nan asked. They were twelve years old and had dark hair and eyes.

"Will it hurt us?" put in blond, six-year-old Flossie. "Maybe we'd better hide."

Her twin Freddie looked worried too. "Is it a very big bug?"

The children were in a corner of the lobby where a pretty Indian girl of eighteen was selling handwoven rugs at a counter. She wore a deerskin dress decorated with colorful beads. Two long black braids hung over her shoulders.

She smiled at the two sets of twins. "Doodlebug is a man."

1

"A man?" they cried.

Just then the front screen door banged shut and a short, white-haired man stomped toward the Indian girl.

"Give me back the things you stole from me!" he demanded, shaking a finger in her face.

Before she could reply, a tall dark-haired man strode over. "I'm Mr. Voss, the hotel manager," he said. "What's going on here?"

"Robin Talltree stole my binoculars and my bird book!" the elderly man shouted. His face was red with anger, and he glared at the girl.

"Oh, Mr. Finn, that's not true!" Robin said.

The Bobbseys were shocked. "I can't believe that!" said Nan. "She's too nice!"

"Robin never stole anything!" declared the young man who had run into the lobby.

Mrs. Bobbsey, a pretty, slender woman, who was registering at the desk, hurried over. A number of other guests gathered. Several spoke out in the Indian girl's defense.

"I have proof!" Mr. Finn declared angrily. He reached into a pocket of his jacket and pulled out a necklace of woven beads.

"Those are mine!" Robin exclaimed.

"You bet they are!" said the man triumphantly. "And you know where I found them? Up in the old Indian lookout across the lake. That's where I left my binoculars and book. I was bird-watching yesterday afternoon and laid them down. There was a crackling noise like twigs breaking on the hill below. This girl was sneaking around in the hazel grove next to my property. She was spying on my place again."

Robin's dark eyes flashed, but she said quietly, "Yes, I was in the grove, but as I've told you before, Mr. Finn, I do not spy on you."

The excited man paid no attention. "I ran down and chased her," he went on. "She made me so mad I forgot to pick up the binoculars and the bird book. When I went back for them this afternoon, they were gone! I found these instead!" He held up the beads.

"I don't wonder you did," said Robin. "I was in the lookout last night, and the necklace must have fallen out of my pocket. I didn't know where I'd lost it. I had seen strange fire in the lookout," she added, "and went to see what it was."

The Bobbsey twins had been listening eagerly. They loved mysteries and this sounded like one.

"This has gone far enough, Mr. Finn," the manager put in. "I've known Robin Talltree a long time and I'm sure she's honest."

He said that the Indian girl had been invited by the hotel to sell her rugs and pottery in the lobby, and also to teach weaving.

"In addition Robin acts as a counselor for children who are staying here. She does an excellent job!"

Mr. Finn's face grew redder. Without another word he tossed the necklace onto Robin's counter and stomped out of the hotel.

Robin thanked everyone. "You were all so nice to stick up for me."

"Who is that man?" asked Mrs. Bobbsey.

"His name is F. C. Finn," the manager replied. "He's a retired engineer, who lives across the lake."

The guests began to move away, and Mr. Voss accompanied Mrs. Bobbsey back to the desk.

Robin gave a big sigh. "I hope nobody thinks I'm a thief. Bleep, you don't, do you?" she asked the young man who had run in ahead of Mr. Finn.

"Of course not. Cheer up, Robin," he said, running a hand through his thick black hair. "Nobody thinks that." He turned to the twins and introduced himself as Toby Bleep. "Just call me Bleep."

The twins told Bleep and Robin their names.

"Bleep is one of the Do-Re-Mees," the Indian girl explained. "They play here every night."

"Wait'll you hear us!" Bleep wiggled his ears, and the twins laughed.

"All kidding aside," Bleep said, "if we're going to clear Robin of suspicion, we must find out who *did* take the doodlebug's things."

"Why do you call Mr. Finn a doodlebug?" Freddie asked.

"Because that's another name for a water witch. In other words, Mr. Finn can find water under the ground with a stick," Robin explained. "The stick is also called a doodlebug."

"You mean Mr. Doodlebug doodles with a doodlebug?" Nan asked, giggling.

"He doesn't look like any bug I ever saw," Freddie put in.

"If you ask me, this mystery's driving us all buggy," Bert remarked. "What this hotel needs is a couple of good detectives."

Freddie stuck out his chest and grinned from ear to ear. "That's us!"

"Yeah?" asked Bleep, raising one eyebrow high. "You could have fooled me."

Bert grinned. "We are detectives, really," he said, and told about a few of the mysteries the twins had solved. "We'll try to find the thief."

"I'd be grateful for your help," said Robin.

"Tell us about the mysterious fire," said Nan eagerly.

Robin explained that the lookout was built of rocks. Near the top was an opening. "Two nights ago I noticed a torch waving in the opening," Robin said. "It was late, so I did not go over to see who was signaling.

"Last night there was no flare, but I decided to investigate anyway. I paddled across the lake and climbed up into the lookout with my flashlight. Nobody was around."

"Were the binoculars and the bird book there?" Nan asked.

"Yes. I saw them lying on the floor, but I didn't touch them."

"Maybe the person who signaled came back today and stole the things," Bert suggested.

"Could be," said Nan. "But who and why?"

"Maybe it was Mr. Doodlebug himself," put in Bleep. "He's a strange old duck."

Robin explained that the retired engineer had moved to the lake the year before. "At first he was friendly, but this summer he suddenly changed. He chases everybody away from his place."

"It sounds as if he has a secret there," said Nan.

"If he has," Bert remarked, "maybe the torch signals and the theft are connected with it. We'd better work on all three mysteries."

Mrs. Bobbsey came over and Nan introduced Bleep to her.

Robin said, "I wish all of you Bobbseys would come over to my house after supper. It's right next door to the hotel."

Mrs. Bobbsey said the twins might go but excused herself. "I'd better unpack," she said.

On the way upstairs she told the children they would have three adjoining rooms. "We can be together," she said, "because two guests were nice enough to move. One of them, Mr. Hobbs, agreed they'd take 310. He'll tell his friend, Mr. Moony, about it."

The twins changed from their traveling clothes, then went down to the lobby to wait for their mother. Robin had left.

Flossie went to a window overlooking the green forests and the blue lake. "This is a bee-yoo-ti-ful place!" she exclaimed. "I'm glad we came to the Poky Mountains!"

"Pocono Mountains," Nan corrected her and added, "I wish Daddy could have come."

The twins' father was at home in Lakeport. His lumber business had kept him from joining the family on vacation.

Freddie meanwhile had noticed that the wooden floor of the lobby was highly polished. Here and there were small, bright-colored Indian rugs.

"I'll bet I could make one of them slide a few inches on this shiny floor," he told himself.

Taking a running start, he jumped onto one of the rugs. Away he went toward the dining room, which was two steps below the lobby.

But he could not stop! WHOOSH! Off the step he sailed, straight into a waitress. She screamed and dropped a tray of silverware! The young woman caught herself on a chair. But Freddie landed, sitting, among the scattered spoons and forks.

The other twins had seen the accident. Bert,

Flossie, and Nan could not help laughing. But now Nan rushed to her small brother. "Freddie, are you hurt?"

"I'm okay," he said, as she helped him up. Freddie turned to the waitress. "I'm sorry. My —my express rug wouldn't stop."

The waitress picked up the rug, then looked into the lobby. "I guess it wasn't your fault, little boy. The cleaning man forgot to put the pad under this to anchor it. I'll report it to Mr. Voss."

Bert was still grinning. "Freddie, want another ride on your flying carpet?" he teased.

"No thanks!"

The twins helped the waitress pick up the silverware, then returned to the lobby. A few minutes later Mrs. Bobbsey stepped from the elevator and they all walked into the dining room, this time properly.

After a delicious supper the twins hurried along the lake front to Robin Talltree's white cottage. It had a wooden dock, with a canoe turned upside down on the boards.

"Hi!" called the Indian girl from her porch.

She led them into a cozy living room. Bright-colored Indian blankets lay across the furniture and were tacked on the walls. A picture of the lake, made of seeds, dried ferns, mosses, and bits of wood hung over a fireplace.

"I made that myself," Robin said. "I gathered

Whoosh!

the twigs and other things in the grove behind Mr. Finn's house. Lots of unusual plants grow there."

The Indian girl explained that she had lived alone in the cottage since the death of her parents a few years before.

"A long time ago my ancestors, the Delaware tribe, settled around this lake and called it Sky Lake because the water is so blue. They used to signal from the lookout with torches. But when the white settlers came, the Indians decided to travel west. When I was born my family moved back here."

She told other stories and served cookies and delicious Indian root beer. Finally the twins said good night. It was dark as they walked back along the beach.

A few minutes later Bert exclaimed, "Look! There's a light in the lookout! Someone's signaling!"

CHAPTER II

MOONY'S MISTAKE

"MAYBE it's an old Indian spook!" Flossie whispered.

"There are no spooks," Bert said quietly, "but I'm sure it's a signal. Let's watch a little longer."

The torch continued to wave back and forth in the window of the stone lookout. In a few minutes it disappeared. The twins waited in silence, but the signal did not come again.

Finally Bert said, "I guess that's that. Let's go!"

"I wonder what the signal meant," Nan remarked.

"I can't wait to go to the lookout," said Freddie.

"And I want to see Mr. Doodlebug again," Nan added.

When the children came into the lobby of the hotel they could hear wild music drifting up from the basement.

11

The young man behind the desk grinned at them. "Everybody's downstairs in the Rec Room listening to the Do-Re-Mees," he explained.

Just then Mrs. Bobbsey came up the steps.

"A very exciting performance," she said with a smile. "Wait till you see what they do with the ladder! I won't tell you. That would spoil the surprise."

"Let's go see it now!" Freddie urged.

"Not tonight," said Mrs. Bobbsey, patting his shoulder. "You'll have plenty of time."

Fifteen minutes later the boys were in their pajamas. But Freddie was not ready to go to sleep. He picked up the pillow from his bed and hurled it at Bert. Plop! It fell on his brother's head.

"So you want to fight, eh?" said Bert and picked up his own pillow. "Look out!"

He whammed it at Freddie, who dodged. The pillow landed on the headboard and the end ripped open. White feathers flew out and snowed onto the bed and floor.

"Uh-oh!" Freddie began to sneeze.

"We'd better quit and clean up this mess," Bert declared.

"Achoo! Achoo!" was Freddie's only reply.

The boys stuffed the feathers back into the pillow and pinned it shut. Bert turned out the light, and in a little while the brothers were sound asleep.

Suddenly they awoke. A key was turning in the door! The next moment it opened and the ceiling light flicked on. In the doorway stood a tall, broad-shouldered man.

"What are you doing in my room?" he boomed.

"This room is ours!" Bert told him.

Freddie pulled the sheet over his head. "I'm going back to sleep."

The man walked toward Freddie, a menacing glare in his eyes. "Oh no, you're not!"

"Hey, you leave my kid brother alone!" Bert cried out.

He jumped from his bed and tried to push the man aside. But the big fellow's hands clamped over Freddie's. He pulled the little boy, the sheet, and the blanket clear across the floor!

To Freddie's amazement the man suddenly dropped his hold. Two shiny shoes met the boy's eyes. He looked up. Staring down at him was the night desk clerk.

"What's all this racket?" he asked.

Bert answered. "This man didn't give us a chance to explain," he said. "You're Mr. Moony, aren't you?" he asked him.

Grudgingly the man nodded.

The clerk said, "There's been a change, Mr. Moony. You're in 310 now."

"What are you trying to pull?" the big man shouted.

Bert replied, "Mr. Hobbs said it was all right. Didn't he tell you?"

"No, he didn't. I just got here."

The visitor stalked out and down the hall in disgust. The desk clerk followed.

The next morning the boys told the rest of their family about Mr. Moony. Freddie added, "He sure was mad."

"I heard the rumpus," said Mrs. Bobbsey, "but I thought it was coming from somebody's TV set." They all laughed.

After breakfast Nan suggested that the twins go down to the Rec Room.

"Oh yes, let's," Flossie urged. "I want to see the ladder."

The children trotted down the stairs into a large, wood-paneled room with a snack bar in the corner. Around the walls were tables with little lamps on them. The center of the room had been left clear for dancing.

There was a small stage at one end of the room. On it stood two guitar cases and a set of drums. A trumpet lay on a chair. A high stepladder stood next to it.

"I still can't figure out what they use that for," said Bert.

Nan was looking into a game room beyond. "I see a Ping-Pong table," she said. "How about a game?"

"What are you doing in my room?"
the man asked angrily

The older twins hurried out, but Freddie and Flossie walked up onto the stage.

"I'll bet it's fun to be on top of that ladder," said Flossie. Suddenly the little girl grinned. "I'm going up!"

She scooted over to the stepladder and began the climb.

"I'm next!" said Freddie.

"No you're not!" came a loud voice. "I am!"

Startled, the young twins looked around and could hardly believe their eyes. A tall, dark-haired boy of Bert's age was striding toward them.

"Danny Rugg!" exclaimed Freddie. "What are you doing here?"

Danny was also from Lakeport and went to the same school as the Bobbseys. He liked to pick on children smaller than himself and especially enjoyed teasing Freddie and Flossie.

"I'm on vacation the same as you, stupid," said Danny, stepping onto the platform.

"We didn't know you were coming to Sky House," said Flossie. She clutched the top of the ladder tightly.

"Course you didn't. You Bobbseys don't know everything," said Danny. "I surprised you—ha-ha!"

With that he grabbed the ladder and began to rock it back and forth.

"Don't do that!" Flossie shrieked.

"Stop it!" cried Freddie and tried to push the big boy away. But Danny only rocked the ladder harder.

"Help!" screamed Flossie.

Bert and Nan rushed into the Rec Room.

"Danny Rugg!" cried Bert. "You cut that out!"

"Make me!" said Danny.

Bert leaped for Danny and tore his hands from the ladder.

At the same time Nan cried, "Flossie, get down! Quick!"

Flossie scrambled to the floor. In the scuffle between the boys both of them lost their balance, knocking the ladder over.

CRASH! BANG! Drums, cymbals, triangles and the two guitars fell down.

"That's all! Knock it off!" boomed a deep voice.

A tall young man with red hair ran across the stage. He jerked both boys to their feet. Bleep and two other young men hurried in behind him.

"What do you think you're doing, anyway?" asked one of them. He wore horn-rimmed glasses and had curly blond hair and a mustache.

"You almost wrecked our instruments!" said another musician, who had long, straight black hair.

As he and Bleep picked up the musical pieces and the ladder, Flossie told them what had happened.

"It's okay," said Bleep. "Nothing's been harmed, but from now on you kids keep off this platform. These instruments are valuable."

Danny snorted. "Valuable! I heard your corny act the other night!" He jumped off the platform and strode out of the room, making faces at everyone.

"As for you—" said the blond-haired man angrily to Bert.

"Cool it, pal," Bleep put in quickly. "These are the twins I was telling you about. They're good kids."

He reached into his pocket and pulled out a white paper bag. "I'll bet you Bobbseys like pistachio nuts," he said. "Have some."

"Thank you," said Nan, taking a handful of the red-shelled nuts. The other twins dipped in too.

He introduced them to the three other musicians. The red-haired man was named Bop. The blond one was Cal and the other Hal.

"I like your funny names," giggled Flossie.

Bleep noticed Freddie staring at his stiff thatch of hair. "You like my topknot?"

Before Freddie could reply, Bleep pulled his bushy hair down over his forehead, crossed his eyes and wiggled his ears. The twins burst into laughter.

The four men grinned. "We musicians have to be different so people will remember us," said Bop.

Bleep changed the subject and asked, "Have you detectives done any work today?"

"Not yet," Nan replied. She told about seeing the flare the night before. "We'd like to ask Mr. Finn what he knows about it."

"I doubt if Doodlebug will talk to you, but no harm in trying," said Bleep.

He told the children they could get a rowboat at the hotel dock and cross the lake straight to Mr. Finn's cabin.

"You'll be lucky if the old grump doesn't throw you in the water," said Cal, grinning at the twins.

Mrs. Bobbsey consented to the trip, but reminded the children they must be back by lunchtime. When they went outside, Danny was leaning against the porch railing. He was talking to Mr. Voss.

The hotel manager looked at the twins with a frown. "You kids will have to learn not to play so roughly," he snapped. "I will not have you making a disturbance in this hotel." He walked stiffly into the lobby.

Danny snickered and ran toward the beach.

"I wonder what he told Mr. Voss," said Flossie. "Ooh, that Danny!"

"It wasn't fair of the manager not to ask our side of it," said Nan. She sighed. "Yesterday he was so nice to us."

Ten minutes later Bert was rowing the others across the lake toward a white dock on the opposite shore. When the boat bumped against the wooden piling, Nan secured it with a rope and the children climbed out.

"Here's a motorboat," Freddie pointed. "And it has FCF painted on it."

"Mr. Finn's initials," Nan said. "This must be the right place."

The twins saw a path that led to a little house and followed it. When they reached the cabin, no one was around.

"Maybe Mr. Doodlebug's in his back yard," Flossie suggested.

The children went around the side of the house and stopped in surprise. The white-haired man was walking away from them, holding a stick shaped like an upside-down Y. He had one prong in each hand with the long point straight up before his face.

Apparently he did not hear the children, nor did he seem to notice a deep gully a few feet in front of him.

"Stop!" Nan cried.

CHAPTER III

THE MONSTER

THE surprised man whirled. "What are you doing here?" he roared at them. "Go away!"

"I was only warning you," said Nan. She pointed to the gully only two short steps away from him.

Finn turned to look, then mumbled, "Thank you."

"How come you didn't see the gully?" Freddie asked curiously. "You were walking right toward it."

"Because I was thinking," the old man said, tapping his head. "Whenever I'm trying to find water I have to think hard about it."

"Don't you have any water?" Bert asked.

"Course I do," the doodlebug replied. "I have a nice deep well, which I found myself with this hazel rod." He waved the forked stick in his hand. "I'm just practicing."

"We didn't mean to interrupt you, Mr. Doodlebug," Flossie piped up. She smiled. "It must be like magic finding water with a stick."

"Lots of people don't believe in it," Mr. Finn said gruffly, "but it works for me."

"I always thought doodlebugs were people who doodled," said Freddie, "—you know, like scribbling things on a pad while they talk on the phone."

"You're right," Mr. Finn replied, "but there are other kinds of doodlebugs. One of them is a real bug." He explained that the bug was the larva of the ant lion.

"What's a larva?" Flossie asked.

"And an ant lion?" Freddie put in.

Mr. Finn told them that the insect was called an ant lion because it ate ants. "A baby insect is called a larva before it grows up to be something else. It's often like a worm."

"You mean if Freddie and I were insects instead of people, we'd love worms?" Flossie asked. She wrinkled her nose at the thought.

"No, Floss, you'd look like a worm!" said Nan, giggling.

Mr. Finn laughed heartily and went on to say, "This ant lion digs a little cone-shaped pit and hides at the bottom of it, waiting for an ant or other small insect to fall in."

"I've seen those pits," said Nan. "They're usually in dry or sandy soil."

The old man nodded. "If you put your head

close to it and call, 'Doodlebug, doodlebug, come out!' the creature will toss up a little sand."

Flossie clapped her hands. "Oh, I want to find one of those!"

Mr. Finn chuckled. "Yes, it's fun to play with them." Suddenly he became quiet. Then he scowled and said, "Why are you children here?"

"We're detectives," said Bert. "We want to find out who took your binoculars and bird book."

"That's no mystery," replied the doodlebug. "It was Robin Talltree!"

"I'm sure she didn't take them, Mr. Finn," said Nan.

"Nonsense!" snapped the man. "I say she did! And another thing, she's always sneaking around the hazel grove spying on me. I don't like people coming here," he added.

Flossie's face clouded. "Does that mean we can't ever visit you again and watch you doodle, Mr. Doodlebug?"

A little smile twitched at the corners of the old man's lips. "Well, I don't mean *never*," he said. "But I don't want you here now. Run along. Scoot!"

"All right," said Nan. "But first tell us, do you know who waves a torch in the lookout?"

"No. And good-by."

Disappointed, the twins left and started for

the shore. "He's a nice man," said Flossie, "when he forgets to be mad."

Nan said, "Before we go home, let's investigate the lookout." But just then the lunch bell sounded across the lake. "We'll have to postpone our trip."

The twins rowed back to the hotel. Their mother was waiting for them on the dock.

"I have a surprise for you," she said. "Robin has invited all the children in the hotel to accompany her to the town of Red Feather this afternoon."

"Oh, that'll be fun!" exclaimed Flossie.

"How many will be going?" Nan asked.

"Only five," her mother replied, leading the way into the dining room. "You twins and Danny Rugg. The other children are busy."

"Ugh—Danny!" said Freddie, making a face.

An hour later Danny and the Bobbseys piled into the hotel station wagon with Robin.

"How far is it to Red Feather?" Nan asked as they sped through the rolling farmland.

"Only five miles," Robin replied. "We're nearly there."

Soon the road leveled out into a street with shops on both sides.

"I have some errands to do," Robin said as she pulled into a large parking lot. "We'll meet here in half an hour."

She pointed down the street to a sign which

read CRYSTAL CANDY STORE. "Take a peek in there. You'll love it." Robin hurried off in the other direction.

The five children started toward the candy shop. Just ahead of them a woman was writing on the sidewalk with a piece of chalk. Alongside her lay a shopping bag and a large watermelon.

"Why, there's lots of writing all over!" Flossie exclaimed.

Danny and the twins edged closer. Scrawled in bold print was, "Harry, meet me at Aunt Jane's house. Mother."

By this time the woman had straightened up and was reaching for the watermelon.

"Did you write all these things?" Freddie asked her.

The woman whirled around, startled, and the watermelon flipped high in the air! Bert was under it in a flash for the catch.

The "football" landed in his arms with such force it sent him backward straight into Nan. She in turn stepped on Freddie's big toe.

"Ouch!" the little boy cried. He held his foot and hopped around right onto Danny's foot.

"You did that on purpose, Freddie Bobbsey!" Danny bellowed, giving him a push.

"I did not!"

"You did too!"

In the confusion Bert returned the watermelon to its owner. By now the woman had regained her composure and was smiling pleasantly. She glanced from face to face and said, "Thank you for rescuing—*your* dessert."

"Ours?" cried the five.

"That's right. I want you all to have this delicious watermelon." She handed it back to Bert.

"Oh, thank you! Thanks a lot. That's cool!" were the happy replies.

As she walked off, the visitors noticed that a narrow path had been left in front of the store so that people could pass by without stepping on the writing.

Along the curb in red chalk were the words, "Let a smile be your umbrella."

At this moment a woman came to the doorway of the candy shop. "Good afternoon, children. I see you're interested in the messages Mrs. Butler leaves here. Everyone in town enjoys the sayings she writes. Once in a while she leaves messages for her son."

"There's not much room left for any more," said Nan.

"Oh, tonight I'll wash the sayings and messages away," the store owner said. "Tomorrow Mrs. Butler will be back with some new ones. Won't you come in? I'm Mrs. Armstrong."

The children followed her into the candy store.

Flossie's eyes sparkled. "Oh, you have everything here!"

Long glass cases full of chocolate chunks, molasses candy, licorice whips, and all kinds of penny candy lined the shelves and counter. A delicious buttery aroma came from an electric popcorn machine against the wall. There was a slot in it for coins and a little door at the bottom which opened when money was inserted.

Mrs. Armstrong excused herself to go to the kitchen. "I have candy cooking," she said.

At once Danny went over to the popcorn machine and began to hit it. "Maybe I can get some free," he said, grinning.

"Hey, don't do that!" said Bert. "You might break the machine."

"That's right," Nan chimed in. "Put in a dime."

"Whadaya mean?" said Danny. "This is an old thing. If you hit it hard enough you don't have to put in any money."

Just then Mrs. Armstrong came back and looked sternly at Danny. He hurried out of the store.

The twins ordered ice cream sodas and sat at the marble counter to drink them. When Flossie finished she slid from her stool and went to buy popcorn. She put in a dime.

At once the door opened. A large paper cup dropped down and popcorn began falling into it. When the container was almost full, she picked it up. But the popcorn kept coming.

"Ooh!" the little girl exclaimed. "Something's wrong!"

Kernels kept flying out. *Pop! Pop! Pop! Pop! Pop! Pop! Pop! Pop!*

Flossie opened her mouth wide and caught three pieces of the popcorn before Bert unplugged the machine and slid the door shut.

Mrs. Armstrong rushed in and shook her head. "I don't know what made it act like that."

The Bobbseys said nothing but they thought it likely that Danny's rough treatment had caused the machine to break.

The twins helped Mrs. Armstrong clean up the mess. She thanked them and gave each one a free bag of fresh popcorn, which they carried to the car together with the watermelon.

They found Danny waiting. Just then Robin arrived with her arms full of parcels. Bert put them in the car, while Nan told about the watermelon. Robin laughed. "Mrs. Butler is odd but a sweet person."

Soon after they started out of town, Robin turned down a side street and pulled up beside a large empty lot. Here and there stakes had been driven in and strings were stretched between them.

"This is some property my father left me," Robin said. "I have given it to the town of Red Feather for a playground. Those stakes and strings mark where the swings and seesaws and other equipment will go.

"Ooh! Something's wrong!" Flossie exclaimed

"But there's one hitch. The town would like to build a swimming pool here. All the water in Red Feather comes from private wells, and we don't know whether there's any water under this property or not."

"Mr. Doodlebug could tell you," Flossie said.

"Yes," said Robin, "but he won't do it."

"Why don't you or the town get somebody else?" Nan asked.

"That would cost money," Robin answered. "People think Mr. Finn should do it free as a citizen of Red Feather."

"Don't worry," Nan said cheerfully. "When we solve the mystery of the binoculars and book, I'm sure Mr. Finn will try to find water for you."

Danny looked disgusted. "Are you kids playing detective again?"

"I'm very glad they're helping me," said Robin firmly.

Outside of town they passed a large sign which read *Red Feather Homecoming Day*. Underneath it were the words, *Enter the Funny Wheels Contest*.

Robin explained that every year many people who had once lived in Red Feather came back for a celebration. "It's great fun," she said, "especially the contest. The idea is to build a crazy car. The funniest and the fastest win prizes. Anybody can enter," she added. "How about you?"

Bert grinned. "Okay, we will!"

"It sounds goony," said Danny.

"Maybe you'll like what we do tonight better," said Robin. "We're going to hike around to the other side of the lake and have a cookout."

By seven o'clock several children from the hotel were seated around a roaring fire toasting marshmallows and playing a guessing game.

"Now it's Freddie and Flossie's turn," said Nan. "You two go out while the rest of us think of a secret word."

Giggling with excitement, the young twins walked a little way into the woods.

"It's kind of dark in here," said Flossie.

Just then they heard a crashing sound in the brush. Next they saw something large and black moving toward them.

"Help!" Flossie screamed as she and Freddie raced back to the fire. "Here comes a monster!"

CHAPTER IV

THE TORCH

"A monster!" Nan exclaimed, jumping up.

"I'm getting out of here!" cried Danny, scrambling to his feet.

As he turned to run, a big black-and-white cow thrust her head from among the trees. For a moment the cookout party was startled. Then they all burst out laughing.

"Here monster, here monster, nice monster," Bert called. The gentle cow ambled over and he patted her. Flossie and Freddie looked embarrassed.

"That's one of Mr. Peter's herd," said Robin. "He has a farm about half a mile from here. Sometimes his cows get out and roam through the woods. He'll be looking for this one in the morning."

"Maybe we ought to take her back now and save him the trouble," Nan suggested.

"That's a good idea," said Robin.

Only Danny and the Bobbseys wanted to go.

"All right," said Robin. "Suppose the rest of you hike back with Donald." He was a local sixteen-year-old boy who had joined the group.

"Come on!" he called. "Let's get going!"

After they had left, Bert said, "If we only had some rope, I'd make a halter for the cow."

"There's a piece in my knapsack," Robin told him.

She reached in and brought out a long coil of hemp. Bert fitted a loop around the cow's neck.

Meanwhile the other children gathered wood for the next picnickers and tidied the campsite. Then they carefully put out the fire.

Robin lit her big battery lantern and started into the woods. Danny, Bert, and Freddie came next leading the cow, then Nan and Flossie. It was dark among the tall trees, so all the children turned on their flashlights.

Presently Nan exclaimed, "Oh! My sandal! It fell off!" She stopped and Flossie paused beside her.

Nan shone her light on the sandal. "Oh dear, the strap's broken. I'll have to find something to fix it."

She flashed her beam around and spotted green tendrils growing up a tree trunk nearby. Nan tried to pull some off.

"Boy, they're tough!" she said.

At last, with Flossie helping, Nan managed to

get a piece loose. Bending down, she tied the broken sandal strap together with the vine.

"Okay," she said, standing up.

"Where are Robin and the others?" Flossie asked in a worried voice. "They've gone."

"Robin was headed this way," said Nan. "They shouldn't be very far ahead. Let's hurry."

She started forward on a run with Flossie at her heels. But after a few minutes, when they reached a clearing, Nan paused.

Flossie asked her, "Are you sure this is the way?"

"Well, I thought it was."

The girls stood listening a few moments. They looked among the trees trying to spot Robin's big light. Through a gap between two pines they could see the old Indian lookout. Beneath it a light was moving.

"Flossie! A lantern! Oh, it must be Robin's!" Nan cried.

The girls shouted at the top of their lungs, "Here we are! Come and get us!"

Instantly the lantern light went out!

"Now nobody can see anything," Flossie complained.

"I wonder why Robin did that," Nan said.

She and Flossie kept calling, but the light did not appear again.

"Maybe that was not Robin," Flossie put in. "Maybe it's the lookout spook!"

"A lantern! It must be Robin's!" Nan cried

"Don't be scared, Floss. We've told you there aren't any spooks. We'll find our way," Nan declared.

Just then they heard voices in the distance. A beam of light swept the trees to their left, and Bert stepped into the clearing.

"Are we glad to see you!" said Nan, heaving a sigh of relief.

"We heard you yell," her twin said. "That's when we realized you were gone. How did you get lost?"

Quickly Nan and Flossie told him what had happened to Nan's sandal and about the mysterious light.

"Hmm," said Bert. "I can't see why the person with the lantern didn't answer you."

"Probably he didn't want anyone to know who he was or what he was doing," Nan said.

"Whoever it is," Bert remarked, "I'll bet he's involved with the Indian lookout mystery."

He led his sisters to the others, who were waiting with the cow. The girls told their story again.

"I'll bet it was Mr. Doodlebug doodling," Freddie suggested.

"He does have a lantern like mine," Robin remarked, "and the hazel grove is near the lookout. One night I was leading a cookout party through there, and we met him."

"What was he doing?" Nan asked.

"I don't know," Robin replied, "because he turned off his lantern instantly and hurried away in the darkness."

"I don't care who it was!" said Danny, shivering. "I want to get out of these crazy woods."

"There's nothing to be afraid of, Danny," said Robin. "First we must take the cow back to farmer Peter."

"I'm not afraid!" retorted Danny. "I just want to get away from here."

Five minutes later they came out of the woods at the edge of a large meadow with cows in it. Straight ahead in the moonlight they saw bars down in the fence.

"Come on, Bossy," Bert said to the cow as he led her up to the break. "You're going in the same way you came out. It's a good thing the rest of the herd didn't follow you."

He took the cow into the field and turned her loose. With a low *moo* she wandered off to join the other cows. Bert came outside again and the bars were set in place.

"Now let's go home," said Robin, and turned back into the woods. "Everybody stay together," she cautioned.

When they came out onto the lake shore they stopped to gaze at the lookout. The top could be seen above the trees. Suddenly a red flare appeared in the window.

"Whee!" cried Freddie. "A torch!"

It began to move back and forth.

"This is a different kind of signal from the one we saw before," said Bert. "It goes from side to side three times and then stops."

Nan added, "Then it does the same thing again."

"Somebody's sending a message!" Bert guessed.

"Let's go up there right now!" Nan said eagerly. "We can see who's doing it."

"I think we'd better not," Robin answered. "It might be dangerous, and we've had enough excitement for one night."

"Oh, please, Robin," Bert put in. "Now's our chance to find out who's signaling!"

"Aw," Danny complained, "you kids are nuts. Let's go back to the hotel."

"You're chicken!" Freddie accused him.

Before Danny could retort, Robin spoke up. "Be quiet, everyone! I know how much you twins want to solve this mystery, but it's getting late and we still have to circle the lake. I am responsible for your safety, and I don't want your mothers to worry."

"All right," said Bert reluctantly. "Maybe we'll see the signal some other time and can investigate it then."

Danny gave the Bobbseys a triumphant look and ran ahead in the direction of the hotel. The twins and Robin followed, still gazing at the tower. The waving torch went out.

"I wonder if the person we saw in the woods was Mr. Doodlebug," Nan said. "And is he the one making the signal from the lookout or is it someone else?"

"I'm sure you'll find out soon," Robin remarked.

When they arrived back at the Sky House the children thanked her for the outing and entered the hotel. Danny went upstairs, but the twins saw their mother in the lobby and stopped to tell her about their adventure in the woods.

"It was spooky," said Flossie, "even if the monster was only a cow."

Bert grinned. "Floss, you missed your chance to have some monster milk!"

"Ugh!" said Flossie. "I'm going to bed."

Freddie was doubled up with laughter. "Don't have any bad dreams, Floss, about cows that have torches for horns."

His twin made a face at him, then she and Nan went upstairs. Bert and Freddie followed and were soon asleep in their room.

In the middle of the night the telephone on a table between the boys' beds rang loudly. With a start they awoke. As Freddie turned on the lamp, Bert picked up the receiver. Before he could say hello, a man's voice spoke.

"You get down to the lobby right away—I need both of you! That's an order!" The caller hung up.

Bert stared at the telephone, astonished.

"Who was it?" Freddie asked. "What did he want?"

His brother told him, then looked at the alarm clock on the bedside table.

"It's three o'clock!" Bert muttered.

"What's it all about?" Freddie asked, bewildered.

"I guess we'd better go see," Bert replied, jumping out of bed and putting on his robe and slippers. "There must be some kind of emergency in the hotel and that was probably the manager calling."

"Why does he want us?" Freddie asked, struggling into his robe and slippers.

"Search me," Bert answered.

Quietly the boys stepped out into the dimly lit hall. It was empty. They walked to the end and pressed the button for the elevator.

After a few moments it arrived and the doors slid open silently. The boys went in, pushed the first floor button and rode down to the lobby. It was dark except for a dim glow cast by the night light over the switchboard.

"Nobody's here," Freddie whispered. He felt suddenly afraid.

"Wait a minute," said Bert softly.

His heart was thumping with excitement. He had been looking at the partly opened door of the manager's office. A flashlight was moving inside the room!

Bert guided his brother quietly across the lobby. They stopped at the open door.

In a beam of moonlight they saw a man in a raincoat and slouch hat kneeling before the hotel safe. He held a flashlight in one hand. The lower part of his face was covered with a black handkerchief.

Freddie gasped. "A burglar!"

CHAPTER V

A STRANGE MESSAGE

HEARING Freddie's voice, the burglar leaped up. He pushed roughly past them and raced out the front door of the hotel.

"What'll we do?" Freddie asked, frightened.

"We can't catch him in the dark," said Bert. "Let's call the manager!"

He hurried behind the reception desk to the switchboard. Seeing a button marked EMERGENCY, he pressed it. Minutes later the elevator doors opened and Mr. Voss in robe and slippers hurried out. His eyes grew large when he saw only the two boys.

"What are you—" he began.

"There was a burglar here!" Freddie exclaimed.

Bert quickly told the story.

"I'll call the police!" the manager said. "Then I'd better get your mother."

Fifteen minutes later Bert and Freddie were

seated on a sofa in the lobby with Mrs. Bobbsey.
The boys were repeating their story to two policemen. One was Officer Sanders, a stout man
with keen blue eyes. The other, named Fritch,
was short and dark-haired.

"It's lucky you boys interrupted the burglar,"
said Mr. Voss. "He would have made off with
the week's payroll. As it is, he didn't even get the
safe open!"

"You have a lot of money in there?" asked
Officer Fritch.

"Yes, right now I do," the manager replied.

Sanders said, "I'm interested in that phone
call to the boys' room."

Mrs. Bobbsey asked him, "Do you think it
was the burglar who called? I can't imagine
why he would want my two boys to come down
to the lobby while he was trying to rob the safe."

"He must have thought we were somebody
else," said Bert. He reminded his mother that
the caller had said, "I need you."

Mr. Voss frowned. "I'm not accusing anyone,
but Mr. Hobbs and Mr. Moony used to have
that room. Maybe the call was for them."

"I think we'd better have a talk with those
men," said Sanders.

The manager telephoned them. Presently they
came into the lobby, sleepy-eyed.

"What's this all about?" grumbled Mr.
Moony.

His companion was a thin man with a sharp nose. He had blond hair which was tousled.

"Perhaps you can tell us about a certain mysterious visitor here," said Officer Sanders. He explained what had happened.

Mr. Moony turned pale, while Mr. Hobbs licked his lips and tried to smile. "We don't know anything about it," he said.

Moony added, "You don't think the burglar was calling us? He could have been phoning any one of fifty rooms in this hotel."

Fritch turned to Bert. "Could you identify the voice you heard on the phone?"

"I don't think so," he replied. "I was half asleep."

"How did the burglar get in?" Mrs. Bobbsey asked.

"The window to my office was unlocked," said Mr. Voss. "He must have climbed in that way."

"It could have been an inside job," Bert remarked. "The door to the office was open."

"I know," said Mr. Voss, becoming red in the face. "The lock is broken. I'll have to get it fixed."

"All right, folks," said Sanders with a sigh. "That's all for tonight, thank you."

The next morning when the Bobbseys seated themselves in the dining room, their waitress Delia greeted them with a big smile.

"Congratulations!" she said to Bert and Freddie. "Everybody's talking about how you stopped the burglary!"

Before the boys could reply, she added, "Did you hear the news? Three other hotels in this area were robbed last night—and all about the same time. Three o'clock in the morning!"

Instantly the twins thought of the torch in the lookout the night before. It had waved back and forth three times. Had it been a signal to the thieves to strike the hotels at three o'clock?

"I'll bet the burglars all belong to one gang," Delia remarked. She took the Bobbseys' order and disappeared.

"I think she's right," said Bert. "Mother, may we row across the lake after breakfast? I'd like to check out that lookout. We might pick up a clue."

Mrs. Bobbsey said yes but warned the children to be cautious. When Delia returned, Bert asked her if she could draw a map showing where the three inns were which had been robbed.

The waitress took a slip of paper from her pocket, then quickly sketched the locations and also included the Sky House.

After breakfast the twins hurried down to the sand beach where a dozen rowboats were lined up. The boat boy gave them one and they headed across the lake. Bert beached the craft and the twins hurried through the woods, avoiding Mr. Finn's property.

Soon they reached the hill that led to the lookout and began the climb. Pine trees grew close together, which made the slope gloomy. Finally the children came out in a clearing at the top. Before them stood a huge circular mound of stones, with a small doorway.

"It's like a big chimney," said Flossie.

"Let's go in," Bert urged.

He led the way through the opening. Dim light filtered down from a hole in the ceiling far above their heads. Crude stone steps curved around the inside wall to the top.

"Better let me try it first," Bert said.

Carefully the children began to climb. At the top they slipped into the small lookout room with the window.

The twins stepped over to the waist-high rock sill and looked out. Below was the sparkling lake with the Sky House on its far shore.

Bert took the map from his pocket.

"One hotel should be over there," he said, pointing to the far left. The children gazed in that direction.

"I see it!" cried Flossie. "There's a red roof among the trees!"

A few seconds later Nan spotted the other two hotels.

"If the thieves are staying at those places they certainly could see the torch signal from here," Bert said.

"Yes," Nan agreed, "but we have no proof. After all, there were flares on two other nights and no robberies then."

"Listen!" Freddie whispered. "Somebody's coming up!"

Footsteps could be heard on the rocky steps!

"Maybe it's the bad men," Flossie said, shivering.

"I'll see," said Bert softly. He peered down through the hole and chuckled. "Robin!"

The Bobbseys called down hello to her and she looked up in surprise.

Freddie asked, "What are you doing here?" as she stepped into the lookout room. "We're detecting."

"So am I," said Robin. She held a paper bag in one hand. "I'm also collecting ferns for my pictures."

Bert told her what the twins suspected about the signaler. The Indian girl agreed.

"But I think we ought to have more proof before you tell the idea to the police."

Flossie touched the paper bag. "I'd like to make a fern picture too. Could we help you go collecting?"

Robin glanced at her watch. "I have to get back to the hotel and give a pottery lesson," she said. "But why don't you collect some ferns yourself and I'll show you how to make a picture." She reached into her jacket pocket and took out two more paper bags.

Freddie shuffled his feet. "I don't want to collect ferns," he complained. "I want to go swimming."

"That's a cool idea," said Bert.

"Suppose you do both," Robin suggested. "Take the long way around to get to your boat."

"How do you do that?" Flossie asked.

"Watch the moss on the trees," Robin said. "It will always be on the south side away from the north wind. From here you go south to the lake and then turn east."

After hunting through the lookout and finding no clues, they all climbed down the stone stairs.

After Robin had left the twins, Flossie ran to look at a tree. "I see moss!" she exclaimed.

It became a game with the children to find their way south to the shore. Presently Flossie gave a cry of excitement.

"Look! A doodlebug!" She scooped the little creature off a leaf into her hand. It was a tiny orange bug with black spots.

"That's a ladybug," said Nan, laughing, "not a doodlebug."

Flossie's face fell. "Good-by, ladybug," she said and carefully put it back on the leaf.

"Listen! Somebody's coming up!"
Freddie whispered

The twins walked on, picked wild ferns and flowers, and put them in the paper bags.

"Oh, my bag is tearing!" said Flossie.

Just then Nan led the way out of the trees into a large cove of the lake. The children stopped short in surprise.

"A houseboat!" Bert exclaimed.

Before them was an old, dilapidated craft. The white paint was peeling off, and the railings around the deck were broken. A heavy brown curtain covered the only window.

"It looks deserted," Nan said.

"Let's knock anyway," Flossie suggested. "Maybe some people do live here, and they could give me another bag."

The Bobbseys crossed the narrow beach and walked up the gangplank to the worn deck. The boards squeaked as the children went to the door.

Nan knocked. There was no answer. She knocked again.

Whack! A hard object hit the wooden wall beside the children.

"Somebody's throwing stones at us!" Nan cried.

CHAPTER VI

KITE BOAT RIDE

"RUN!" cried Flossie as another rock hit the door of the houseboat.

The twins dashed from the deck onto the narrow beach and ran into the woods. After a few yards they stopped.

"Who do you suppose was throwing stones at us?" Flossie asked.

"I don't know," Bert said, "but I'm going to find out!"

The girls slipped to the edge of the trees and peered into the cove. Mr. Hobbs was standing on the other side of the houseboat. The next moment he disappeared into the brush.

"You think he was the one?" asked Freddie, who had followed his brother.

Bert shrugged. "I don't know. Why should he care if we knocked on the door of the houseboat?"

The two girls had also seen Hobbs and were

puzzled. He would have had no reason to harm the Bobbseys.

"Maybe it was Danny playing a trick," Freddie suggested.

Nan shrugged. "Well, I guess nobody lives here," she said. "If he did, he would have come out by now with all that noise."

"Oh!" said Flossie suddenly. "My paper bag! I lost it!"

"You dropped it on the deck of the houseboat," Nan told her. "I'll get it for you."

While the others watched from the trees for the stone thrower, Nan hurried across the beach and onto the old craft. As she picked up the brown bag, something bright caught her eye. Lying in a crack on the deck was a beautiful yellow feather.

"How pretty!" Nan thought, lifting it out. "We can use that in one of our pictures." She ran back to the others. "Here, Floss, see what I found."

"Oh, isn't it bee-yoo-ti-ful!" the little girl exclaimed.

Bert said, "It must be nearly lunch time. We'd better start back."

When they reached the Sky House, Mrs. Bobbsey was on the porch with Robin. While Flossie showed them some of the treasures they had collected, Nan told about the houseboat and someone throwing stones at them.

"Maybe it was Mr. Doodlebug," said Freddie.

Robin frowned. "He isn't very friendly, but somehow I can't believe he'd throw stones at you. By the way, that old houseboat has been deserted for years."

After lunch the children put on bathing suits and went down to the beach.

"We have to wait half an hour before we can go in the water," Nan reminded the others.

Just then a big spurt of sand flew into her face. "Ow!" she cried.

The others looked up to see Danny Rugg standing nearby. He smirked.

"Sorry. My mistake," he said.

Bert's eyes sparkled angrily. "You didn't make another mistake today, did you?" he asked. "Like throwing stones at us?"

Danny looked blank. "I don't know what you're talking about." He walked off, scuffling sand.

"Do you think he was telling the truth?" Flossie asked.

"He didn't sound as if he were fibbing," Nan said.

When the half hour was up, Bert said, "Why don't we take our swimming and canoe tests now? Then we can all go in the kite boat."

"In the what?" Flossie asked.

Her brother pointed down the shore to a small

dock. An odd-looking craft was tied to it. The sail was stretched like a kite over a big rectangular framework. This hung in a U-shaped rigging.

"When the wind lifts that sail," Bert explained, "it pulls the boat along."

"It sounds like fun," said Nan.

The children hurried over to a sun-tanned, muscular young man standing beside a high wooden chair. He was wearing bathing trunks with the word LIFEGUARD written on the side. Nan asked if the twins might take their tests.

"Right away," he said. "You can call me Ken," he added, and led them to the water.

The twins were good swimmers, and each had had some experience in canoes. In a little while the lifeguard had passed them all.

"Now may we go in the kite boat?" Flossie asked him.

Ken glanced around and saw that the beach was becoming crowded. "Yes, but not until my assistant arrives to cover for me here. I'll meet you at the boat in half an hour."

When the time came the twins headed down the beach. They noticed a young woman in slacks standing beside the kite boat. She wore a red kerchief over her hair and had on sunglasses. As the twins drew near, she turned and walked away.

A few minutes later Ken caught up to the children. "All set?" he asked. "Who knows how to sail a boat?"

"I do," Bert answered.

"Then you'll have no trouble," said the guard. "Just do what I tell you." Bert listened carefully as Ken instructed him how to handle the two-seater boat. "You'll need someone for a crew," he added.

"Oh, let me go," Flossie begged.

"Okay," said Bert.

He lifted his little sister into the bow seat and settled himself in the stern. Ken gave the boat a powerful push into the water. As Bert took the tiller, the wind caught the square sail.

"Here we go!" cried Flossie, when the craft skimmed out onto the lake.

The wind blew harder and the boat raced away. The Bobbseys were almost flying!

Suddenly they heard two loud cracks, one after the other. The sides of the wooden rigging had broken!

"Look out!" cried Bert as the sail fell.

Flossie screamed. The framework had struck her. The boat capsized and both children were tossed into the water.

"Flossie!" Bert gasped as he came up.

His little sister was not in sight. He dived quickly and spotted her blond hair. Grabbing one of her arms, he pulled her to the surface.

"Are you okay?" he asked, treading water and holding her up beside him.

After a moment Flossie's eyes opened. She coughed and spluttered, then took a deep breath.

"I'm all right," she whispered.

Moments later the lifeguard was beside the children in a canoe. He helped them to shore, then paddled out again and towed in the kite boat.

"Whatever happened?" Nan asked him. "How could the kite break like that?"

Ken's face was grim. "Somebody sawed this rigging almost all the way through," he said and added, "It was okay before lunch."

"What a mean trick!" said Freddie.

"It was worse than mean. I'll report it to the manager," Ken said, "and try to find out who did this."

He turned to Flossie and patted her wet head. "I think you have had enough lake for today," he said. "All of you better go back to the hotel."

They walked to the dock and started for the hill. When they passed the beachhouse Freddie exclaimed, "Look!"

Someone had chalked a message on the side wall. It read:

BOBBSEYS GO HOME—UNLESS YOU WANT
MORE TROUBLE LIKE THE KITE BOAT.

"So that wasn't just a mean joke," said Nan.

"Look out!" cried Bert

"Somebody knew we were going in the boat and wrecked it on purpose!"

Bert looked grim. "I didn't notice anybody near it except that girl in slacks."

"Maybe Ken knows who she is," Bert said. He ran down the beach to the guard, who was dragging the broken kite boat away from the water. Bert asked him about the girl.

"That is Miss Leaf," Ken replied. "She's been at the hotel a week, but she's very quiet and keeps to herself most of the time. Do you think she might have tampered with the boat?"

Bert shrugged and returned to his brother and sisters. "Her name is Miss Leaf," he said.

"That's a funny name," said Freddie, chuckling.

The children rubbed the message off the wall, then went up the hill and directly to their rooms.

"Another message!" exclaimed Nan, when she opened the girls' door. She picked up a paper on the floor. "It's from Mother," she said. "There's going to be a funny hat contest in the Rec Room in half an hour. We have to make our own."

"Out of what?" asked Freddie.

"Anything," said Nan. "The kookier the better!"

Fifteen minutes later the girls had showered and dressed. Quickly Nan put a large lampshade on her head upside down, then tied it on with a long scarf.

"Now me," said Flossie. "I want a turban." Nan wound a big blue towel around Flossie's head.

"I want my feather on it!" the little girl exclaimed.

"Okay," said Nan. She stepped to the dresser and looked into Flossie's paper bag.

"It isn't here," she said, shaking her head. "You must have lost it."

Flossie's face fell. "Oh dear! It would have looked so nice."

"Never mind," said Nan. "We'll stick something else on your turban." She picked up a bunch of pink tissues, made a long paper feather from them, and pinned it on the front. "Now you have a plume!"

"Oh it's bee-yoo-ti-ful!" Flossie said, looking at herself in the mirror.

The girls hurried down to the Rec Room. Guests with odd hats were milling about and the Do-Re-Mees were playing loudly.

"Mother!" Nan exclaimed, seeing Mrs. Bobbsey in a corner.

She was wearing an upside-down flower pot on her head. Sticking out of the hole at the top was a bright red geranium.

"Oh, Mommy, yours is funny!" Flossie cried.

"Not so good as yours," said her mother, laughing.

Just then the girls saw Freddie wearing a sand bucket for a helmet. "I'm a tin soldier!" he announced as they walked over to him.

Bert arrived with a red shirt wrapped around his head like a bandana. "I'm a gypsy," he said in a deep voice.

Bleep rolled the drum and called for quiet. At that same moment Danny walked up to the twins. Flossie's eyes grew wide as she stared at the feather on the front of his white turban.

"Danny Rugg!" she exclaimed. "That's *my* feather! You give that back!"

CHAPTER VII

THE ZOO CLUE

"I will not give it back!" Danny retorted. "I found this feather on the porch!"

As his voice rang out in the quiet room, the guests turned to look at the children.

"I guess you must have dropped it there, Flossie," her sister whispered. "Just forget it."

"It's mine now," Danny added loudly.

"That's enough!" cried Mr. Voss, coming over to them.

"These Bobbseys are trying to take part of my hat away from me," Danny declared.

"No, we're not!" Nan exclaimed.

"Now listen to me," said the manager crisply. "You twins will have to learn to get along with Danny. I don't want quarrelsome children in this hotel."

Before the surprised Bobbseys could answer, he walked to the platform.

"Ladies and gentlemen," he said over the mi-

crophone, "will you please parade past the
judges." He nodded toward three hotel guests
seated beside the platform.

While the Do-Re-Mees played, the contes-
tants marched around the room in their outland-
ish hats. Then Mr. Voss stepped forward again.

"The judges' decision is that Mrs. Bobbsey
wins the prize for the ladies," he announced.
Everyone clapped and the twins cheered. "Mr.
Bronson wins for the gentlemen."

A short fat man wearing a pink baby bonnet
walked to the platform with Mrs. Bobbsey. Mr.
Voss gave each of the winners a big straw hat.

"As for the five children," the hotel man went
on, "the judges thought all their hats were so
good that they are giving out equal prizes. Each
child may go to the snack bar for a free ice
cream stick. And day after tomorrow, Robin
Talltree will take them all down the Delaware
River on an overnight canoe trip. The treat is on
the hotel!"

As the audience applauded, the Bobbseys
beamed. Danny, however, grumbled. "It's not
fair. My hat should have won first prize."

That evening it rained and the twins played in
the game room. The Do-Re-Mees had no performance. Afterward the children sat at the big
window in the lobby and talked.

"I have a riddle," said Nan. "Who knows
what a dowser is?"

Flossie gazed at the rain. "It's when you get doused."

"No. Guess again."

Freddie thought it was a man who worked a crane on a truck. Bert said, "Is it a hose?"

Nan laughed. "You're all wrong. A dowser is a water witch—like Mr. Finn."

"He has lots of names," said Flossie. "Let's go see him again. I want to watch him find water."

"Good idea," Bert agreed.

Next morning after breakfast the Bobbseys rowed across to Mr. Finn's dock. As they walked up to the cabin, they saw him come out of the woods with an armful of branches.

"Hello, Mr. Doodlebug!" called Flossie.

"Hi, Mr. Dowser!" said Freddie.

Startled, the man looked over. "Get out!" he yelled. "I don't want you here!"

Flossie stopped short, and her eyes filled with tears. "But we only wanted to talk to you," she said.

"We're sorry, Mr. Finn," Nan added. She took Flossie's hand. "Come on, dear. We'd better go."

"We thought you might be willing to help us with our detective work," said Bert.

"Well, I'm not."

"He didn't have to be so mean about it," Freddie burst out.

Mr. Finn heard him and his face grew red.

"I'm not mean!" he exclaimed, as the children turned to leave. "All right! Wait a minute!"

The old man disappeared behind his house. When he came back a moment later, he no longer had the wood in his arms.

"Now what is it?" he asked, frowning.

"We wanted to ask about the old houseboat in the cove," said Nan. She told him what had happened there.

"For goodness sake!" he exploded. "You think *I* threw stones at you?" Then he added with a sigh, "I can't blame you. But I didn't."

"We believe you," said Nan and the others echoed her.

"As for the houseboat," he went on more cheerfully, "nobody's living there. I understand that old wreck has been empty for years. Course, men sometimes come to the lake for night fishing and sleep in the houseboat. The old tub is safe enough. She stays afloat." He looked thoughtful. "I can't see any reason for anybody to throw stones at you, though."

"We found a pretty feather on the houseboat," Flossie put in. As she described it, the old man's blue eyes sparked with interest.

"Sounds like a golden pheasant's. Only place around here that feather could have come from would be Gibson's Game Farm—it's a sort of zoo."

"Get out!"

"Oh, maybe Robin would take us there!" Freddie exclaimed.

The doodlebug's face darkened. "Stay away from that girl! It's plain as day that she took my bird-watching stuff. And what's more, I think she's the one who's sneaking around here at night and lighting flares in the lookout."

"Oh, I'm sure you're wrong, Mr. Finn," said Nan earnestly, "because Robin was with us when—"

"Nonsense!" the man interrupted. "I'm one hundred per cent right!" With that he turned on his heel and strode into his cabin.

"We may as well go back to the hotel," said Nan with a sigh.

The twins found their mother playing Ping-Pong with Robin. They told her what had happened at Mr. Finn's place and about the game farm.

"Could you take us there?" Nan asked Robin.

"Glad to. We'll go after lunch."

"Danny, too?" Freddie asked.

"Yes," said Robin with a smile. "He's a hotel guest, too, you know."

But when she invited him at lunch, the boy said he did not want to go. Other children had to refuse, too, because of previously made plans.

Afterward the twins and Robin set out in the station wagon. As they wound down the road Bert noticed a blue sedan behind them. He spotted it again as they drove through Red Feather.

A mile beyond the town Robin pulled into a gravel parking lot in front of a large fenced-in area. Over the entrance gate was a sign, GIBSON GAME FARM. The Indian girl bought tickets at a small booth and led the twins into the zoo.

A tall man wearing overalls and a wide-brimmed straw hat was throwing hay over a fence to some deer. "Howdy, Miss Talltree," he said with a grin. "You bringing another group to see my game farm?"

"Yes, Mr. Gibson, but these children are special," she replied. "They're detectives." She introduced the Bobbseys.

"Well, I could use detectives," said the man grimly. "My office was robbed three nights ago."

The zoo owner told the callers that the thieves had stolen money from his safe. "They also took several bunches of feathers."

"Feathers!" exclaimed the twins.

"Yes," Mr. Gibson replied. "Our peacocks and golden pheasants have beautiful feathers. We collect those that they drop and sell them at the souvenir stand."

"Golden pheasants?" said Nan. "Then a feather we found might be a clue to your burglars!" As Mr. Gibson looked puzzled, Nan told about the houseboat.

The zoo man shook his head doubtfully. "It's

more likely some child from the Sky House dropped that feather."

"Yes," Robin agreed. "There were lots of children at the hotel earlier this summer. I brought them here and they all bought souvenirs."

At that moment Flossie saw a cage of white rabbits near the ticket booth.

"Oh, may we pet the bunnies?" she asked.

"Go right ahead. Take a couple out," said Mr. Gibson.

While Robin talked to the zoo owner, the twins went over to the cage. Bert took two rabbits out and gave them to the young twins.

"Hold them carefully," Nan said as Freddie and Flossie ran their hands over the soft fur.

"Listen," said Bert eagerly. "Do you realize that this game farm was robbed the first night we saw the flare in the lookout?"

Nan nodded. "I'll bet the same men who robbed the game farm robbed the hotels."

"And someone signals from the lookout when the jobs are to be done," Freddie added.

"Maybe," said Nan, "they use the houseboat for a hideout."

"And maybe Mr. Hobbs is one of the gang," put in Freddie excitedly, "and threw the stones at us 'cause he didn't want us to find his hideout."

Flossie gave her rabbit an excited hug. "We've solved the mystery!"

"Let's tell the police!" said Freddie eagerly.

"Not so fast," Bert replied. "We don't have one bit of proof."

"No, we mustn't accuse anybody until we're sure," said Nan.

"All right," said Flossie. She chuckled as she put the rabbit back in its cage. "Nobody heard us but the bunnies and they won't tell anybody."

Robin came over just then and told the twins she had errands to do in Red Feather. "I'll meet you at the front gate of this place in an hour."

The twins strolled around the zoo for a while.

"There are the peacocks!" said Nan, spotting the big birds stalking gracefully about their wire pen.

One of them raised its long tail feathers and spread them wide in a blue and green shimmering fan.

"He's bee-yoo-ti-ful!" Flossie cried.

"Look at this fancy chicken," exclaimed Freddie at the next cage. He was pointing at a bird with many colored feathers—red, blue, orange with black stripes, and a golden-yellow crest.

"That's not a chicken—it's a golden pheasant," Bert said. "See the sign."

"The feather Nan found was just like the ones in his topknot," said Flossie.

The twins walked on, then stopped at a souvenir stand. Flossie and Freddie chose plastic monkeys on sticks to buy, and the older twins purchased peacock feathers for their mother. When they met Robin, she told them that they were going to eat at a nearby church supper.

"Mr. Gibson told me about it," she explained. "I've called your mother and she says it's okay."

The five ate a hearty supper under the trees at long tables. For dessert they had warm home-made apple pie with ice cream.

"That was yummy," said Flossie as they started home. It was nearly dark as Robin drove up the mountain road to Sky House.

They had not gone far when a boy darted into the beam of the headlights. He signaled wildly for Robin to stop.

CHAPTER VIII

FALSE ALARM

"HELP!" cried the boy on the road. Robin stopped the station wagon beside him. "There's a man in the woods and he's hurt!"

"What's happened?" Bert asked.

"Come on!" the boy urged, moving toward the trees. "Hurry!"

"Okay," Robin agreed, pulling the car over onto the shoulder of the road. "Nan, you stay here with the young twins and lock yourselves in. Bert and I will see what the story is."

The Indian girl took her flashlight from the glove compartment. Then she and Bert followed the red-haired boy into the woods.

Flossie looked out the window anxiously. "I wonder what happened to the man."

They all watched the trees for a while. No one appeared. After a few minutes Freddie began playing with the two rubber monkeys the young twins had bought at the game farm. Flossie laid out the peacock feathers and smoothed them. Suddenly the red-haired boy dashed from the woods.

"Come on!" he called breathlessly. "They need you."

"The man must be badly hurt," said Nan as the children piled out of the station wagon, leaving the doors unlocked.

They hurried after the strange boy, and almost had to run to keep up with him. Through the deep gloom they could see his white shirt moving ahead of them. Soon he paused and pointed to a small hill.

"In back of that," he called. "Go there!" The next moment he dashed off in another direction.

"Where's he going?" asked Freddie.

"Maybe to get more help," Nan guessed.

The children rounded the hill and found themselves in a small clearing. No one was in sight.

"Robin!" Nan called. "Where are you?"

"Here!" came the Indian girl's voice. "Where are you?"

"In the clearing," Freddie yelled.

The next moment a flashlight bobbed among the trees. Bert and Robin appeared.

"What are you doing here?" Bert asked.

"The boy said you needed us," Nan replied.

Bert frowned. "We didn't send for you."

"Where's the man who was hurt?" Flossie asked.

"I don't think there is any," said Bert. "It was a false alarm. Something's fishy about this whole thing." He explained that the red-haired boy had pointed out a big oak and told them that the injured man was lying under it. "Then the kid ran away."

"And there was nobody under the tree," Robin added.

Nan told how the boy had led her and the young twins to the hill.

"I'm afraid we've all been tricked," Robin said. "We'd better hurry back to the car."

She had a good sense of direction and led the Bobbseys straight to the road.

When Flossie climbed into the back seat, she cried out in dismay. "Our souvenirs are all spoiled!" The plastic monkeys had been cut into pieces and the feathers were broken.

"That's a shame," Nan said.

Bert picked up a piece of paper from the front seat. Robin shone her flashlight on it.

"It's a note," said Bert. Printed in pencil were the words:

YOU KIDS MIND YOUR OWN BUSINESS OR ELSE!

"I think we're getting even closer to solving the mystery," said Nan. "Whoever left this warning must be worried about our hunt for the thieves."

"In that case," said Bert, "I think it's time we tell the police what we suspect about the lookout and the houseboat."

Robin agreed. "But let's not mention Mr. Hobbs or Mr. Moony. After all, it isn't fair to name people without any proof." She slid behind the wheel. "There's a State Police headquarters on the highway. We'll go there right now."

She turned the station wagon around and drove down the mountain. A short distance outside Red Feather, Robin pulled up in front of a one-story brick building.

Inside, the Bobbsey party found Officer Sanders at a desk with several telephones. He recognized the twins at once. Quickly Bert introduced Robin and told what had happened on the mountain road.

"Who could have known you were going that way?" Sanders asked.

"I don't know," Bert replied. "But someone may have followed us from the hotel to the Game Farm." He told about the blue sedan he had noticed.

"If that person had eavesdropped on Robin and Mr. Gibson," Bert went on, "he would have learned we were going to the church supper before riding back to the hotel. There would have been time enough to set up the trap."

The officer asked Robin if she had noticed anyone standing close to her while she talked with the Game Farm owner.

"I don't remember anyone special," the girl replied, shaking her head. "There were a number of people walking past and some standing nearby feeding the deer." Nan told the policeman the children's suspicions about the hotel thieves, the houseboat and the lookout.

"That's an interesting idea," said Sanders, "and we'll check out those locations. But I don't want you to get your hopes up," he added kindly. "For one thing, lots of vacationers like to signal from that lookout just for the fun of it. Every year we have so many reports about it that we don't even bother to investigate them any more."

As the twins looked downcast, he went on, "I don't want to sound like a spoilsport, but even if you're right about the lookout, I'm afraid it's too late to catch the thieves there."

"Why?" Bert asked.

"We think they've moved their operations to the town of Calico about fifty miles north of here. There were several daring robberies at that place last night."

"But if the gang has left here, why would they

bother to warn us to mind our own business?" Nan asked, puzzled.

"Maybe they didn't," the officer replied. "Somebody else might be playing a joke."

The Bobbseys thought of Danny, but none of them believed he would do a trick like this.

"Well, don't worry," Sanders went on. "We'll look into the matter tomorrow."

The next day was Sunday and the Bobbseys attended early services in a small church near the hotel. Afterward the twins and Danny and Robin piled into the station wagon. A trailer with two canoes on it was hitched to the rear. Mr. Voss took the wheel and as Mrs. Bobbsey smiled and waved, they drove off.

After an hour's ride they pulled into a clearing beside the wide, sparkling Delaware River. Both canoes were carried to the water's edge. One pack of camping gear was put in each craft. Mr. Voss told the children to have a good time with Robin, then drove off.

"I'm not going to paddle with girls," Danny announced.

"Okay," said Bert. "You and I can go in one canoe and take Freddie with us. The girls can have the other."

"Suits me," said Flossie, tossing her head.

Soon the two craft were skimming along on the blue water. They passed green fields and rolling hills on either side. As the sun became hotter Freddie let his hand trail in the cool foaming water.

After a while Bert noticed that the canoe kept swerving sideways. "Hey, Danny," he called over his shoulder, "what are you doing?"

Freddie glanced back. "He's not doing anything."

"I'm resting," said Danny. "It's too hot to paddle."

"Let me do it awhile," said Freddie.

"All right," Danny agreed. "Come on! I'll change seats with you." He started to get up. The canoe rocked wildly.

"Sit down!" Bert cried. "You want to dump us in the river? Everybody knows you shouldn't change places in a canoe."

"I don't need any orders from you," Danny grumbled.

"Cool it, fellow," said Bert. "We'll be stopping soon for lunch, then you can change places."

Fifteen minutes later Robin headed her craft for a dock in front of a gray farmhouse. Over the screened-in porch was a sign:

AUNT SADIE'S FISH PLACE.

It was cool inside the house. After freshening up, the travelers took seats at a large table with a red-checked cloth.

Everyone ordered fish sandwiches, french fries, and milk. There were several other customers around the room.

"Tonight we'll sleep at Yellow Pine Camping Grounds," Robin said as she passed the ketchup to Bert. "We should reach there about five o'clock."

Danny groaned. "Can't we go home? I'm sick of this trip."

"You knew you'd have to paddle when you agreed to come," Robin reminded him.

"But I'm tired," Danny whined.

"Let's take a vote," said Bert. "How many want to go home? Raise your hands."

Only Danny put up his hand.

"Guess you're stuck, Danny," said Bert. "We go on."

"I'm not going," said Danny. "I'll take a bus or something back."

"Indeed you will not," said Robin firmly. "You came with us and you're staying with us. Besides, there is no bus near here."

Danny glowered at his plate, but finished every bit on it. For dessert he had the same as the others—a chocolate sundae.

"I don't feel good," he muttered.

"Maybe you ate too much," Nan suggested.

"It's not my stomach," said Danny. "My head hurts."

He was the first to leave the table and went to

"Sit down!" Bert cried

the candy counter next to the cashier. As the twins looked over, they saw Danny pay the cashier, put something into his pocket and go outside.

After Robin had paid for the lunches, the twins strolled out to the riverbank with her. Danny was not in sight. They called, but he did not appear.

"We'd better look for him," Robin said, frowning.

The five went off separately, calling his name. As Flossie was passing the front of the restaurant she suddenly heard loud groans coming from the porch. She went up the steps and peered through the screen door. Danny was lying in a lounge chair.

"What's the matter?" Flossie asked. "We've been looking all over for you. Didn't you hear us calling?"

The boy did not answer.

Flossie opened the door and stepped onto the porch. She paused and gasped.

"What happened to you, Danny?" she cried. "Your face is full of red spots!"

CHAPTER IX

SURPRISED CAMPERS

DANNY groaned again. "I'm sick," he said weakly.

Flossie hurried outside and called loudly for Nan and Robin. In a moment they came around the corner of the house, followed by the boys.

As they dashed up the porch steps Flossie cried, "Danny's sick! Look at his face! It's full of spots!"

Freddie burst out, "Maybe he has the measles!"

Robin went over to Danny and put her hand on his forehead. "I'm terribly sick," he said. "You'll have to take me back to the hotel."

"You have no fever," said Robin, puzzled.

"Wait a minute," Nan spoke up. She had been looking closely at Danny and sniffing. "I don't think he's sick at all. I smell cinnamon."

"You're right!" said Robin, putting her

hands on her hips. "Danny Rugg, what have you been doing?"

"He's been spotting his face with cinnamon drops, that's what!" said Bert.

"You go wash your face," said Robin sternly.

"The spots won't come off," Danny whined. "They're real."

Robin's eyes gleamed. "You want us to wash them off for you?"

"Never mind," said Danny quickly. He got up from his chair and stomped off to the washroom.

While he was gone Freddie thought, "We ought to play a trick on him."

He scooted off and captured a small frog at the edge of the water. When Danny returned and was about to step into the canoe, Freddie slipped up behind him and dropped the frog down inside Danny's tucked-in shirt. At once the boy began to dance around and grab at his back.

Bert and the girls had seen Freddie's trick. They burst into laughter and Bert teased, "The measles make you itch, Danny?"

The tormented boy yanked his shirt out and the frog plopped into the water. Danny glared at Freddie. "I'll get even with you for this!" he declared.

The campers continued their trip. The sun was turning the water to a golden color when they pulled ashore again at a wide clearing.

Here and there were small stone fireplaces. At one side was a narrow dirt road leading into the woods. A sign on a tree said:

YELLOW PINE CAMPING GROUNDS.

"I guess we're going to be alone," said Robin, noting that there was no one else around.

Packs were unloaded from the canoes, and two tents pitched close to the trees. Then the visitors unrolled the bedding.

Freddie looked at the flat, waterproof sleeping bags. "These are hard beds," he said.

"You have to blow 'em up," Bert told him. Using a small bicycle pump which had been brought along, he inflated all the bags. "They'll be nice and soft now."

After the sleeping bags had been put in the tents, a flashlight was placed on each one.

"I can't wait to crawl into mine," said Flossie.

Soon hamburgers were sizzling over the open fire while the campers munched potato chips. After eating, they sat around the embers and Robin told stories. Gradually it grew dark. Flossie fell asleep and Nan suggested they all go to bed.

While the boys and Robin put out the fire, Nan led her sister to the girls' tent. She opened the flap, felt for a flashlight, and turned it on.

"Oh!" Nan cried in dismay. "Our sleeping bags have been slashed!"

The others hurried to look. After inspecting

both tents, they found that all of the inflatable bedding had been cut with a knife and was now flat.

"Who would have done such a thing?" Robin asked indignantly.

"Somebody must have crept up through the woods," said Bert, "and slit the bags while we were sitting around the fire."

"Hey, look!" cried Danny as his flashlight swept the side of the boys' tent. In large black letters someone had printed:

BOBBSEYS GO HOME!

"Another warning!" exclaimed Nan.

"The bad men again!" cried Flossie.

Bert frowned. "Who could have found out we're here?"

Robin looked puzzled. "I didn't say where we'd camp until we were having lunch at the restaurant. Did one of you tell anybody?"

As she spoke, Bert's light shone on Danny, whose face grew red.

Bert said, "Okay, Danny, did you tell?"

"I didn't mean any harm," the boy muttered. "After I bought the cinnamon drops some little guy stopped me on the porch. He asked where we were going to camp tonight."

"A little man!" Nan exclaimed. She exchanged looks with the other twins and Robin. Could it have been the small burglar?

"Another warning!" exclaimed Nan

"What did he look like?" Nan asked.

Danny shrugged. "I don't know 'cause he had on big sun glasses. He was wearing a straw hat and a colored sports shirt. I never saw him before."

"Well, one thing is sure. We can't stay here tonight," said Robin. "It isn't safe. We can walk to the highway and I'll phone Mr. Voss to come and get us."

"But what about the canoes and all our gear?" Bert asked. "We shouldn't leave it. Someone might take the stuff."

"That's right. Well, we'll paddle back to a house where I know people named Brown. We can leave the things there."

Everything was packed, and the disappointed campers set off again. The Browns' boathouse was only half a mile away. Fortunately it was unlocked. The equipment was stowed inside.

The campers walked up a lane to the house. Though there were lights in the house, no one answered the doorbell. Robin and the children started up the highway in the moonlight.

"Listen!" said Nan presently. "I hear singing!"

The next moment a large open truck came around a curve of the road. The back was full of hay with about twenty children perched on it, singing.

"Wait! Stop!" called the Bobbseys, waving their flashlights.

The driver pulled over to the side of the road. "What's the matter?" he asked.

Robin explained briefly.

"Climb up on the truck," the man said cheerfully. "We're from Camp Arrowhead, but we can drop you off in Boonville."

The friendly campers helped the Bobbsey party climb up into the hay. On the ride they all sang songs together. When they reached the town, the truck stopped in front of a drugstore.

The driver called back, "You'll find a telephone in there."

The Bobbseys, Danny, and Robin scrambled down from the hay, then thanked the driver and the children. Robin hurried inside the store and called Mr. Voss. At ten o'clock he arrived in the hotel station wagon.

"You were wise not to stay at the campsite," he said.

"The trip was too long," Danny complained. "I had a terrible time. It was all the Bobbseys' fault."

"I don't see why you twins can't get along with Danny," said Mr. Voss.

"It isn't our fault," said Nan.

"I really don't think it is," Robin put in.

"Well, maybe not," said Mr. Voss irritably,

"but I don't want to hear any more about it."

The Bobbseys said nothing, but all of them were puzzled by his unfair attitude.

It was midnight when the campers reached the hotel. Mrs. Bobbsey was waiting.

"I was so worried when I heard what happened," she said. "After this you must be extra careful."

The Bobbseys were up early next morning and hungry for breakfast. Afterward they talked to Robin, then Bert suggested that the twins look for the Do-Re-Mees.

"Wait until they hear what happened to us!" said Freddie.

As the children hurried into the Rec Room they were surprised to see officers Sanders and Fritch with Mr. Voss and the musicians.

"More trouble!" Bleep said to the twins. "Our guitars have been stolen!"

"How dreadful!" Nan exclaimed. "When did it happen?"

"It must have been late last night or early this morning," said Bop, "because the instruments were there when we went to bed."

"We checked the hotel and the grounds," said Officer Sanders. "There's no sign of the instruments and no clues. By the way," he added to Bert, "yesterday we searched the places you suggested. We found nothing of interest. Certainly no one is hiding out on that houseboat."

A few minutes later the police left with Mr. Voss.

Hal sighed. "Cal will have to go back to the city right away and rent two guitars. But they won't be the same as the stolen ones. Ours were specially made to take a beating in our performance. It's kind of wild."

"I can't wait to see it." Bert grinned.

"Let's look for clues to the thief," Nan suggested. "We might be lucky and find something the police missed."

"We want to help," Bleep offered.

Bert said, "Suppose Bop and Flossie and I search around the hotel. Nan, you and Bleep and Freddie take a rowboat and go across the lake to search in the lookout."

The detectives separated. In a little while Nan's team was entering the lookout. Quietly they searched the ground floor, then climbed the rocky steps and pulled themselves into the room at the top. They found nothing.

Bleep looked glum and pulled a white bag from his pocket. "Have some pistachios," he said.

The children helped themselves. While they munched the nuts and looked out the window, Nan told the musician about the canoe trip.

She had just finished when Freddie seized Bleep's sleeve and pointed down. Sneaking around the base of the lookout was a small man in a straw hat and a bright-colored sports shirt!

"Just like the fellow who questioned Danny at the restaurant!" Nan whispered.

Bleep's eyebrows shot up, and he thrust the bag of nuts into his pocket.

"I'll follow him," he said softly, "and see what the guy's up to. Meanwhile, you keep watch for anybody else sneaking around in the woods. If I'm not here by the time the lunch bell rings, you row over to the hotel. I'll hike back."

Swiftly he lowered himself through the hole and the children heard him scrambling down the steps. They looked at the lake and the woods for a long time. Then Nan suddenly spotted something flashing among the trees on the hill below.

"That's in the hazel grove," she said softly. "Come on, Freddie, let's investigate!"

The two made their way down to the grove. Suddenly they heard the crackling of twigs. Someone was moving among the trees just ahead! The children quickly stepped behind a clump of bushes to watch.

"I need more—always more!" said a voice. The doodlebug's!

With large shining shears, Mr. Finn was cutting hazel twigs from a tree. That was what the Bobbseys had seen gleaming in the sun!

A moment later he turned and spotted them.

With a startled cry he dropped the branches and the shears.

"What are you doing here?" he shouted. "I told you not to spy on me!"

Nan opened her mouth to reply, but the angry man ran toward them, his arms waving. "Go away!"

Frightened, Nan and Freddie raced down the wooded hill. They could hear the doodlebug coming too and yelling.

As Nan dashed from the trees at the bottom of the hill, she forgot about the deep gully. Suddenly it was in front of her! She took a huge leap and got across.

"Freddie, look out!" she called back.

She saw him jump wildly through the air. He missed the far edge and dropped into the gully.

CHAPTER X

THE PINCHING BUG

NAN dashed back to the gully. To her surprise Freddie was sitting on a pile of branches.

"You're not hurt?" she asked.

"No, I'm okay. I landed on these." He bounced up and down. "They're springy."

"Those are hazel branches," said Nan as she helped her brother crawl out of the gully.

"Where's Mr. Doodlebug?" the little boy asked worriedly, glancing toward the woods.

"I don't know," said Nan. "I guess he gave up chasing us." After a pause she added, "That's funny. A lot of these branches are broken."

She and Freddie pulled out several and examined them. "It looks as if someone tried to hollow them out and they split," Nan remarked.

"Do you think maybe Mr. Doodlebug did it?" Freddie asked.

Nan shrugged. "It seems a funny thing to do."

Just then the lunch bell sounded across the water loud and clear.

"I'm hungry," said Freddie. "Let's hurry back. Bleep said not to wait for him."

The two children dropped the hazel branches back into the gully and jogged to the shore. By the time Nan and Freddie reached Sky House, lunch was being served.

They quickly washed, then joined the rest of the family in the dining room. Robin was sharing a table with them. Quickly Nan reported what had happened with her detective team.

"You did better than we did," Bert remarked. "We didn't find any clues."

Robin said she wondered what Mr. Finn had meant by always needing more hazel branches. "All he has to do is cut a new green branch whenever he's ready to look for water."

"Maybe he needs a lot because the sticks break when he tries to hollow them out," Nan suggested. "Perhaps he's trying to put something inside."

Bert said, "I'd like to know what Bleep found out about the man he was trailing."

"Poor Bleep!" said Flossie. "He'll be so hungry when he gets here! He has to walk all the way around the lake and only has nuts to eat."

They all waited anxiously for him, but the musician had not returned at suppertime. Hal,

Cal and Bop stopped at the Bobbseys' table to talk over their friend's absence.

"Maybe he picked up a clue and the trail was too hot not to follow," Bert suggested.

"Maybe, but he knows we have to play tonight," said Bop, looking worried.

Bleep did not come back. The Bobbseys went to the Rec Room to watch the Do-Re-Mees. Although the young men played cheerfully, the performance suffered without Bleep's clowning and the ladder stunt.

When the Bobbseys came down to the lobby next morning the first people they saw were Bop, Hal, and Cal. They were talking to the manager.

"Did Bleep come back?" Bert asked them eagerly. The men shook their heads.

"The police have just left," said Mr. Voss. "Half a dozen officers searched the woods thoroughly, the houseboat, and the lookout. There's no sign of Bleep anywhere."

Mrs. Bobbsey frowned. "That's a shame. Children, I don't like the looks of this. Today I want you to stay around the hotel."

The twins agreed, disappointed and concerned about their friend. After breakfast Bert went to the gift shop and bought a pencil and pad of white paper. Then he sat in the swing on the porch and began to draw.

"What are you doing?" Flossie asked him.

"I'm sketching an idea for the Funny Wheels contest."

"Oh boy," said Freddie, "what's it going to be?"

"Uh-uh, no peeking," his brother replied. "I want to surprise you."

"Okay," said Flossie. She hopped down from the swing and skipped off the porch. "I'm going to look for a doodlebug!"

"I'll help you," Freddie offered.

A few minutes later Nan came outside and sat down on the steps with her paper bag of mosses, leaves, and seeds. "I hope I can make a nice picture out of these," she told Bert.

The twins amused themselves for a while, then went swimming with their mother. At lunch Bert announced that his Funny Wheels sketch was finished, but he wanted to talk to somebody about it before telling his family.

"You sure are mysterious," Nan said.

In the meantime Flossie had gone to the gift shop and bought a small box of peppermint candies. She poured them out on a clean tissue, twisted it tight and stuck it in her pocket with the candy box.

"Now I have a bug box," she told herself happily. "When I catch my doodlebug I'll put him in here." She hurried to the yard and started looking again.

After an hour Freddie went to the waterfront

to take a diving lesson. When he arrived Danny was playing in the water.

"Okay, Freddie," said the lifeguard. "Go up on the low board and do as I tell you."

After a while there was a shrill ring from inside the beach house. "That's the phone," said Ken. "I must answer it. You two boys come out of the water while I'm gone."

As he hurried off, they swam ashore, but immediately Danny ran over to the high diving board.

"Hey, come on up, Freddie," he said, climbing the stairs.

"No, thanks." Freddie started to build a sand castle.

"Aw come on!" Danny called down from the board.

"I'm busy," Freddie replied. For a few minutes he patted the damp sand into place.

Suddenly Danny gave a yell. "Ouch! My foot!"

Freddie looked up, shading his eyes. Danny was sitting on the edge of the diving board, holding his foot and making a terrible face.

"I can't get down!" he cried. "You'll have to come and help me!"

Freddie hesitated. "Are you sure it isn't a trick?" he asked.

"Oh, please!" Danny pleaded. "Come on! It hurts!"

Freddie went over and climbed up to the board.

"Wow! It's way high over the water here!" he thought as he walked carefully out toward Danny.

"Give me your hand and I'll help you get up," Freddie said, leaning over the boy.

Danny grinned and gave him a hard push. With a yell Freddie fell off the board. But in the nick of time he took a deep breath, grabbed his nose and put one hand high over his head.

SPLASH! He hit the water and went straight down. Kicking wildly, he fought his way to the surface. He came up unhurt and took a deep breath. Danny climbed down the ladder to the beach laughing.

"I'll get you for that!" Freddie yelled and began to swim for shore.

At this moment the lifeguard came from the beach house. Danny did not see him. Ken reached Danny just as Freddie splashed ashore.

"Okay, Danny, I saw you push Freddie!" he said angrily.

Danny turned in surprise. His face grew red, as Ken ordered him off the beach. "And stay off for the rest of the day," he said.

Scowling, Danny turned and scuffled through the sand toward the path that led to the hotel.

Freddie finished his diving lesson, then hurried up to the Sky House. When he entered the lobby a little later he found the older twins with his mother and some other guests. Flossie came skipping through the front door.

"I found a doodlebug!" she called happily and ran over to her family.

Flossie opened one end of the box and shook it. Into her hand rolled a large black bug.

"Eek!" Nan squealed. "Drop it, Flossie!"

Frightened, Flossie threw up her hands and the bug and box dropped to the floor.

"Why? What's the matter?" Freddie asked.

"That's a pinching bug," said Nan. "See the pincers at the front of his head? He could have nipped you, Flossie."

The little girl made a face.

"You'd better put him outside again," said Bert. He took the box from Flossie and pushed the bug inside with a pencil.

Holding the box well away from her, Flossie carried it onto the porch and dumped the bug over the railing. "Good-by, pinching bug," she said. "I want a doodlebug."

That evening Mrs. Bobbsey took the twins and Robin to the movies at Red Feather. While waiting for the box office to open, the children went to Mrs. Armstrong's candy store. She was glad to see them again. "Having fun?" she asked.

"Yes, and lots of 'citement," Flossie answered. She and Nan were the last to leave the shop.

Danny gave Freddie a hard push!

"Look over there!" said Nan.

Across the street was a girl wearing a full skirt, sun glasses and a kerchief on her head. She carried a large tote bag. As the girl walked off, the Bobbseys noticed that she was not very tall and had big knobby knees.

"Sort of like a boy's," Flossie whispered.

"I think that's Miss Leaf," said Nan, "but I'm not sure because we didn't see her close enough at the waterfront."

The sisters paused to look over the chalked messages on the sidewalk.

"There's a funny one," said Flossie. Someone had written:

MEET HIM IN CALICO CAT.

"I wonder what it means," Nan remarked.

"Oh, look!" said Flossie, pointing to the theater. "The people are going in."

Bert called to them to hurry. The girls ran **up** the street and followed the rest of the family into the movie house.

When the first feature was over, the children went to the refreshment stand in the lobby to buy colas. Nan was last in line. As she waited her turn, she saw the girl with the tote bag come out of the box office. The girl carefully closed the door behind her and hurried out to the street.

"She acts kind of sneaky," Nan thought.

On a hunch she walked over to the box office

and knocked on the door. There was no answer. Nan turned the handle and peered inside.

The cashier was on the floor!

"Oh!" Nan gasped, and stooped beside the man. "He's unconscious!" Then she saw that the cash register was open and empty!

CHAPTER XI

PET SHOP UPROAR

"WHAT shall I do?" Nan wondered. She thought of the crowd in the theater and decided to act quietly. "I don't want to get everyone excited."

Quickly Nan picked up the phone in the box office and dialed the operator. "Please send the police to Red Feather Movie House right away. There's been a robbery." Then she left the box office and closed the door.

Loud music from inside the theater told her that the second picture was beginning. People began to go back to their seats. As soon as the lobby was empty, Nan told the woman behind the refreshment counter what had happened.

The clerk gasped and ran to the box office. Nan hurried into the theater and whispered the story to her mother who had an aisle seat. Minutes later the Bobbseys and Robin were in the lobby.

"It's Mr. Colt, the manager," said the refreshment clerk anxiously. "I hope he's not hurt badly."

Robin and Mrs. Bobbsey rubbed the man's wrists, and his eyes fluttered open. Bert helped him sit up.

"I'm all right," he said, "but oh my, have I got a headache!"

Just then officers Sanders and Fritch arrived. Mr. Colt told them that he had heard the door of the box office open behind him.

"As I turned around, I saw a girl wearing sun glasses and a scarf over her hair. She hit me on the head with something and I blacked out." He sighed. "Usually I keep that door locked. But tonight I was careless."

Meanwhile Bert and Freddie had dashed out to the street. Possibly they could find the thief.

"There she is!" said Bert.

In the dim glow of a street light they saw her dodge down a side street. The boys sprinted after her as she dashed into an empty lot.

"That's the playground Robin gave the town!" Freddie exclaimed.

The small figure ahead darted this way and that, leaping over the low strings which had been staked out to mark the places for equipment. Suddenly she tripped and fell flat.

"Now we've got her!" cried Freddie, running ahead.

"Watch out!" Bert called, but Freddie's foot caught on a string and he fell.

Bert stumbled over his brother and hit the ground beside him. Meanwhile the thief raced into the woods beyond the lot.

The boys got to their feet and looked off into the darkness. "We've lost her," said Bert in disgust. "And you know what? I'll bet she's not a girl. She ran just like a man."

"It looked like that Miss Leaf," Freddie replied.

The boys returned to the movie theater and told their story to the police.

"So you think it's a man in disguise," said Officer Sanders. "Got any other ideas?"

The twins all thought of Miss Leaf but decided not to name her until they were sure that she and the thief were the same person.

"Well, you've done a good job again, children," said Fritch. He patted Nan's shoulder. "Especially this young lady who thought quickly and acted quietly so there was no disturbance in the movie house."

After the policemen had gone, Mrs. Bobbsey suggested that they all return to the hotel. "You've missed so much of the picture, it wouldn't be worthwhile going back in."

On the way home the twins talked of nothing but the thief. Nan said, "I'm sure that girl is the same little man who tried to rob the hotel and also questioned Danny."

"Probably," Bert agreed. "And cut up our sleeping bags, and maybe he's the one Bleep followed into the woods."

"Poor Bleep," said Flossie.

For a little while no one said anything as they thought about the missing musician.

Finally Nan spoke up. "You know, Flossie and I saw the thief in front of the candy store. Maybe one of the sidewalk messages was for him."

Flossie put in, "One of them said, 'Meet him at Calico Cat.'"

"There's a little town called Calico," Mrs. Bobbsey remarked.

"Yes," Bert said, "and Officer Sanders said the police thought the gang had moved there. Maybe if we go to Calico, we can find them."

Mrs. Bobbsey smiled. "I'll take you to Calico tomorrow morning. But remember this. If we see the thief, don't try to catch him. We'll report him—or her—to the police."

The twins promised.

When the travelers reached Sky House, Bert and Nan went straight to the desk and inquired about Bleep. The clerk looked worried and shook his head. "No word yet. We can't understand it."

Nan asked about Miss Leaf. "We'd like to meet her," she said.

"Miss Leaf's not in yet," the clerk replied, glancing toward the mail rack. "See, her key is still in her box."

The next morning Nan and Bert inquired again if Miss Leaf had returned.

"No," the clerk said. "She didn't come in last night. The chambermaid tells me her bed has not been slept in."

The older twins thanked the man and left the desk. "I'm sure 'she' has gone to Calico!" said Nan. "If we could spot the thief there for the police, he might lead them to Bleep."

The ride took the Bobbseys over bumpy country roads and narrow bridges. Finally they came into a small town which looked very much like Red Feather. As they got out of the car, Flossie gave an excited cry and pointed a short distance down the street.

"There it is! The Calico Cat!"

Hanging over the door of the shop was a large sign. On it were the words THE CALICO CAT and a picture of a blue cat with white spots. The twins hurried up the street, while Mrs. Bobbsey paused to lock the car.

"It's a pet store!" Freddie cried excitedly.

The windows were full of kittens. "I guess they specialize in cats," Nan remarked.

As Bert opened the door a bell tinkled. A tall, pale-faced man with blond hair hurried out of a back room.

"What can I do for you?" he asked.

While the young twins looked around at the counters piled high with cat baskets and boxes of animal food, Bert asked politely, "Are you the owner of the store?"

"Yes, I am. Did you want to buy something?" The man spoke impatiently.

"No, thank you," said Nan. "We're looking for someone. Has a young woman, carrying a big tote bag and wearing a scarf over her head, and sun glasses been here?"

"No, and there's nobody here now," said the man crisply.

Freddie and Flossie had gone over to see a long row of animal cages on a shelf.

"Oh, look, here's a raccoon!" said Flossie. "Isn't he darling?"

The bright-eyed creature stood up on its hind legs and peered at the little girl.

"See how he holds onto the bars with his little paws," Flossie said. "They're kind of like hands."

Freddie spotted a small perch lying nearby on the shelf. He picked it up and poked the stick through the bars. "Here, raccoon, hold this."

Instantly the animal grasped the stick and yanked it into the cage.

"Hey, he took it away from me!" Freddie exclaimed and laughed.

With that the raccoon hit the stick hard against the outside latch of the cage.

"Don't do that!" Freddie cried, alarmed when the latch flew up.

Before he could put it down, the raccoon pushed the door open and leaped out.

"Stop! Come back!" Freddie called as the raccoon scrambled to the next shelf.

Using his paws deftly, the little animal opened six cages, one after another! From each one leaped three or four cats!

"Oh, no!" exclaimed Flossie. She waved her arms wildly. "Go back! Go back!"

"Freddie! Flossie!" said Nan.

The pet shop owner gave a cry of dismay, but it was too late. By now there were cats all over the store! Some leaped onto the birdcages and others ran across the counters. One landed beside the fish tank and put her paw down toward the goldfish.

Meanwhile three or four cats raced to the front window and another sat on top of the cash register. As the Bobbseys and the pet store owner chased them, the cats meowed and yowled.

Just then a small man in sun glasses came out of the back room of the store. He was carrying a black valise with holes in it. As he hurried past the leaping, running cats the man kept his head

"Go back! Go back!" Flossie cried

down. He opened the front door quickly, slipped out and almost ran into Mrs. Bobbsey as she came in. Then he sped down the street.

"Who was that?" Nan asked the pet store owner excitedly. "The man who just went out?"

The owner did not answer the question. Instead he said angrily, "You children get out of here!"

"We're very sorry about the cats," Nan said quickly, "but—"

"Please let us help you catch the kitties!" put in Flossie.

"You heard me!" the man cried. "Get out of here before I call the police."

"Just a minute," said Mrs. Bobbsey. "What's the trouble?"

"Trouble enough!" the owner cried. "These kids have made a shambles of my shop!"

Freddie said, "We offered to put everything back, but he won't let us."

Mrs. Bobbsey finally got the story straight. She made the small twins apologize and offered to pay for any damage.

The owner of the Calico Cat said sternly, "I don't want any money. Just get out of here, all of you!"

Without a word the Bobbseys left the shop and walked up the street. Bert said sadly, "Mother, I think we nearly caught Miss Leaf, but he got away. He was the one who almost knocked you over."

"He?" his mother asked.

"Yes. We think Miss Leaf is really a man and he was the one."

"It's too bad you lost him," Mrs. Bobbsey said. "How about our having some lunch?"

She spotted a sandwich shop and they went inside. After they had ordered, Nan said, "You know the pet store owner told us a fib, Mother. He said there was nobody in the place, but that little man must have been in the back room all the time."

Bert nodded. "It's hard to believe the store owner didn't know he was there. Maybe that cat man is part of the gang!"

A waitress brought their cheese sandwiches and fruit drinks. The Bobbseys had just finished, when the shop door opened and a tall policeman stepped in. He looked over the customers, then walked up to the twins and their mother.

"Are you the Bobbseys?" he asked.

"Yes, sir," Bert replied.

"Come with me, please," the officer said.

CHAPTER XII

NUTSHELL TRAIL

FREDDIE'S heart sank. He thought that the pet store owner had sent the officer to arrest the twins.

"It's all my fault," he said shakily. "I'm sorry about the cats."

"I don't know anything about cats," replied the policeman who said his name was Yorky. "You are to return to Sky House right away."

"What has happened?" Mrs. Bobbsey asked.

The officer explained that Mr. Voss had called the Calico police and asked that the Bobbseys be found and sent back.

"What's the matter?" Nan asked, worried.

"The State Police are organizing a search for the musician Bleep," Yorky told her. "Some of the guests in the hotel are going to help. Robin thought you twins would like to be there, too, so she asked Mr. Voss to send for you."

"I'm so glad she did," said Bert.

"She told Mr. Voss you were good detectives." Yorky grinned. "Were you over here on—er—business?"

"Yes," Flossie answered. "We saw a man in the pet shop. But the other day he was a girl."

Yorky laughed. "So you're after a masquerader, eh?"

The twins told the officer the whole story. At the end Mrs. Bobbsey said, "We don't want to accuse an innocent person, but this small man is certainly acting strangely."

The officer nodded. "I think I'll have a talk with the pet shop owner. He's new in town. Bought the business from a man who retired and went to California to live."

Mrs. Bobbsey paid the lunch bill and hurried to the car with the twins. Robin was waiting for them at the hotel parking lot. As they walked inside, she said, "I'm so glad you got the message and came back. This mystery just couldn't be solved without you."

Freddie thumped his chest importantly. "Course not," he said.

The twins told Robin about their adventure in Calico.

"A little man in the pet shop!" she remarked. "I'm glad you told the policeman about him."

Robin now explained that the starting point for Bleep's search was to be the Sky House. When they reached the porch, they found many of the guests and Mr. Voss gathered there. At one side they spotted Mr. Finn. In a few moments several policemen arrived, led by Officer Sanders.

He called for quiet and then unrolled a large map of the area. He divided the searchers into groups of three. Each team was assigned to one part of the woods.

Mr. Finn and Bop were given the section around the cove. "Very well," said the doodlebug nervously, "but I don't want anybody trespassing on my property."

Officer Sanders looked at him, steely-eyed. "We're searching everywhere, Mr. Finn."

The other man bit his lip and nodded, but the Bobbseys could see that he was unhappy at the thought of people poking around his place.

"You twins take the lookout," said Sanders. "My men have combed it thoroughly, but you can check it again for clues. Mrs. Bobbsey," he added, "we need one more to go to Peter's farm, but maybe you'd rather stay with your children."

"I'm sure there's no danger for them with the woods full of people," said Mrs. Bobbsey. "I'll go with the farm team."

"Thank you," said Sanders. "My men will take everyone across the lake in the two hotel motorboats. When you've finished searching your section, walk around the shore to the hotel. Keep close watch all the time!"

The twins were assigned to the first boat. When they reached Finn's dock, the Bobbseys scrambled out and hurried to the top of the hill. Once more they slowly and carefully searched the first floor of the lookout, then each step and finally the top room. They found nothing. They came outside again and began to examine the ground.

"Hey, look!" said Freddie. He stooped and picked up something red. "A pistachio shell!"

"Great, Freddie!" Nan exclaimed. "Bleep *was* eating nuts the day he disappeared."

"That's right," said Bert. "Let's see if we can find some more."

Flossie clapped her hands. "Let's everybody spread out and start looking." She got down on her hands and knees.

In a few moments the little girl called, "Here's one!" She held up a red shell.

"And here's another!" Nan exclaimed, as she walked deeper into the woods. Straight ahead was a narrow trail.

"I'll bet Bleep went this way," Bert said.

Taking the lead, he walked down the shady path. Now and then the twins found a pistachio nut shell, but no other sign of the missing musician. Once or twice they heard voices in the distance as other teams called to one another.

After a while Bert looked up at the sky and saw that the sun was slanting toward the west. "It's getting late," he remarked.

"Everything's so quiet," Flossie said softly. "I don't hear anybody calling any more."

"No, I guess they've all started back to the hotel," said Bert.

"We must be way past the cove," said Nan. "Down near the south end of the lake."

"We'd better hurry," Bert urged.

The children continued along the narrow path until at last it stopped short at a big jumble of rocks.

Just then the twins heard a groan and shivered a little in fright.

"What was that?" Freddie whispered, clutching Bert's arm.

"It sounded as though it was coming from among those rocks," his brother replied softly.

As quietly as they could, the twins climbed onto the huge rock pile. The muffled groan sounded again.

"Somebody's down there!" Bert whispered.

He pointed ahead to a deep ravine partially hidden by a rocky roof.

"I'll go down," he offered. "I'm not afraid."

"Be careful," Nan said as her twin lowered himself feet first through the wide crack.

For a moment he hung by his fingertips, then

"Somebody's down there!" Bert whispered

dropped lightly several feet to the bottom. Another groan came from a little distance away.

His heart beating hard with excitement, Bert peered through the gloom. He saw a figure propped up against the wall.

"Bleep!" Bert cried and ran forward. The musician was tied, gagged and blindfolded.

"He's here!" Bert called to the others.

Nan helped the young twins down into the ravine, then followed. Meanwhile Bert removed Bleep's blindfold and gag and untied him.

"Oh, thank you!" the musician said, rubbing his ankles and wrists. "I thought nobody'd ever find me!"

"Who did this to you?" Bert asked.

"Three men, but I don't know who they are," said the young man hoarsely. "I was following that little fellow through the woods and saw him climb over these rocks and disappear. I came up after him and fell into the ravine." Bleep made a face. "I dropped right into those men's laps!"

"But you didn't see their faces?" Nan asked.

The musician shook his head. "No, they jumped me almost as soon as I hit the bottom. Then the men blindfolded me and tied me up. I could tell by their voices that there were three of them."

"Maybe you could identify them that way for the police," Bert suggested.

"I'm afraid not," said Bleep. "They talked in

whispers. I heard the name of one, though. It's Ivy. I know he's the fellow they meant, because someone said, 'Ivy's a little shrimp, but he's smart.'"

"So the small man's name is Ivy," said Bert. "Well, more than ever, I'm sure he's also known as Miss Leaf."

Nan chuckled. "They sort of go together— Ivy and Leaf."

"If you ask me," Freddie spoke up, "he's Poison Ivy." The other twins laughed and even Bleep grinned weakly.

"Are you hungry?" Nan asked him anxiously.

"No, they gave me food and water. But I sprained my ankle when I fell down here. I'm afraid I can't walk very well."

Bert looked up at the steep sides of the ravine. "We'll need help to get you out."

"We'd better go for it quickly," said Nan anxiously. "Ivy and the others may return."

Freddie looked worried. "But everybody's gone back to the hotel. It will take hours to walk there."

"Mr. Finn should be home by now," said Bert. "He can help us."

"Good idea," said Bleep.

"Freddie and I'll get him," Bert declared. "But I think Nan and Flossie should hide in the woods and keep an eye on the ravine. If the men come back the girls can get a good look at them."

"Okay," said Bleep. "But you kids be sure to stay hidden. Those three fellows are rough."

With Bert's help the young twins and Nan were boosted out of the ravine. Then they reached down to give their brother a hand. The girls hid behind a clump of brush nearby, as the boys started to jog through the woods.

Using the sun as a guide, Bert headed for the lake. After a while they spotted the blue water. When they paused, panting, Bert said he thought they should go to the cove first.

"Maybe Mr. Finn and Bop are still searching there."

The brothers hurried along the waterfront and soon reached the cove. No one was in sight. The setting sun cast a rosy glow on the peeling white paint of the houseboat.

"Mr. Finn and Bop may be inside," said Bert.

The boys made their way around the edge of the cove and stepped onto the deck. The next moment there came a deep, spooky *twang* from inside the houseboat!

CHAPTER XIII

MYSTERIOUS BASEMENT

"THAT'S a spooky noise!" Freddie said softly.

The next moment a shout came from the woods. Bop and the doodlebug were walking out.

"What are you doing here?" Bop called.

"Looking for you," Bert replied.

Forgetting the weird sound from the houseboat, the boys ran ashore. Bert told Mr. Finn and Bop about finding Bleep. They were thrilled.

"You'll need a rope to get him out," Freddie added.

"Okay," said the doodlebug. "I'll run back to my house and get one." He trotted off into the woods.

The others waited anxiously for his return. Soon he arrived carrying a coil of old rope.

"I'm afraid this is not very strong," he said, "but it's all I have."

"It'll have to do," said Bop. "Let's go!"

Bert and Freddie led the way to the pile of rocks. No one was in sight.

Bert gave a low whistle. The next moment his sisters appeared from behind the trees.

"Did the men come back?" Bert asked anxiously.

"No," said Nan. "But just the same I think we'd better hurry."

Quickly the rescue party climbed over the rock pile. Bop looked anxiously into his friend's gloomy prison.

"I'm here with a rope, Bleep!" he called. "We'll have you out in a minute!"

"Thanks."

Bop and the doodlebug tied one end of the rope around a big boulder and dropped the other end into the ravine.

"I'll go down and tie it onto Bleep," Bert offered.

"I'll go with you," Nan said.

"All right," replied Mr. Finn. "But take it easy on that rope. It's kind of worn in spots."

"Don't need it going down," said Bert.

He dropped into the ravine, then caught his twin as she followed. They helped Bleep limp to the rope. The children fastened it carefully under his arms.

"It's lucky you don't weigh much," said Nan.

"Okay, pull up!" called Bert.

As he boosted Bleep, the two men at the top hauled him out.

Swiftly they untied the rope and dropped it back down to the twins. While Bert and Nan climbed out, Bop talked to his injured friend.

"Wait'll I get those thieves!" he said angrily. "They had a nerve kidnapping you."

Bleep managed a weak grin. "I don't think they meant to keep me very long," he replied. "The little one said they'd have to hold me prisoner until after they pulled off the big job, otherwise I'd spill the beans. They thought I overheard them planning it, but all I heard was that they mean to blow up a safe somewhere."

"I guess they were afraid you might identify them," said Nan.

"What was the big job?" Freddie asked.

Bleep shrugged. "I don't know."

"Never mind all that," said Mr. Finn. "We'd better get Bleep back to the hotel."

"That's right," said Bop, "and we'll send some police out here in case those thieves turn up again."

"I don't think it's any use tonight," said Bleep. "The men never come after dark."

Bert suggested that he and Nan stay behind to check the ravine for clues.

The old man and Bop looked doubtful, but finally Mr. Finn said, "All right, but don't stay long. The rest of us will take Bleep back to the hotel in my motorboat. Nan, you and Bert go to my house and wait. When I come back I'll take you across the lake, too."

Bert and Nan thanked him.

"It's all right to sit in my kitchen," he said. "I don't want you waiting out in the woods with a gang of thieves running loose. And lock yourselves in," he added.

Bert and Nan lowered themselves into the ravine again with the rope.

"The daylight's going fast," Bert remarked. "We'd better search quickly."

The twins made their way into the darkness under the rocky roof, feeling the sides with their hands and scuffling their feet along the earth.

"Wait a minute," said Nan. "Here's something by the wall." She picked up a heavy object. "It's a pair of binoculars, I think."

The children stepped over to a shaft where the light was brighter.

"You're right," said Bert.

The glasses were in a leather case with a strap. On the lid were the initials F.C.F. "These are the doodlebug's!" he exclaimed.

"This proves the gang took his binoculars," Nan said. "I can't wait to show them to Mr. Finn."

Bert put the strap of the case around his neck, and the twins made their way back to the rope. As Nan started to climb up, she glanced above and saw that the worn strands had rubbed against the rough stone and were fraying. The next moment the rope snapped. With a cry she dropped back into the ravine.

As she hit the bottom Bert caught his sister and steadied her. "Are you hurt?" he asked.

"No, but now our rope's broken."

"That's okay," said her brother. "I can climb up without it and give you a hand."

At this instant the rumble of voices came from above and the sound of heavy shoes on the rocks. The twins exchanged frightened glances. Bert pulled Nan back into the shadow of an overhanging rock.

"We must get out of here somehow," he whispered. "No telling what those men might do if they find us."

The next moment a pair of large legs appeared over the edge of the ravine and a big man dropped down. His back was turned to them.

The twins did not wait to see more. As quietly as possible they inched their way forward in the darkness. At the far end where they had found the binoculars, Bert pointed to jagged rocks leading upward. Nan knew that he meant they could climb out that way.

"What's this?" hissed an angry voice. "A rope! Somebody's been here!"

"And the musician's gone!" whispered a second man.

"Shh!" said a high thin voice. "There may be somebody around."

Quickly Bert gave Nan a boost and she began to climb up the rough face of the ravine. Her brother followed close behind. As she passed a thorny bush growing from a crack in the rocks she felt a sharp jerk on her head.

"Ow!" she cried softly. Her hair was caught!

Seeing his sister's plight, Bert edged past her and scrambled up over the edge of the cleft. Lying flat, he reached down and swiftly untangled her hair. Then he grasped Nan's wrists and with a mighty heave pulled her out. The next moment they were crawling quietly over the rocks.

"I'm afraid they heard me," Nan whispered, "and my plastic headband—it caught on the thorns and it's still there."

Suddenly behind them they heard a cry of rage.

"I'll bet they've found it," said Bert. "Come on! Run!"

As the twins dashed into the woods they realized that running would make too much noise. Bert took his twin's hand and pulled her around behind a clump of brush so they could hide.

Hardly daring to breathe, the children watched, but no one appeared. They heard loud crashing in the brush as the men raced off in another direction.

Nan's hair was caught!

"Now," said Bert, "let's make a dash for Mr. Finn's house."

The children ran through the darkening woods. When they reached the doodlebug's cottage, there were no lights inside.

"He's not back from the hotel yet," said Nan.

They hastened around to the kitchen door, found it open and went in. Bert locked the door behind them. Then he took off the binoculars and laid them on the table.

The kitchen was gloomy. "I'd like to put on a light," said Nan uneasily, "but I don't think we should. If those men come around they might guess we're here."

"We'd better just sit and wait," said Bert.

The twins settled themselves on chairs. Then they noticed a ticking sound. Bert glanced across the room to the cellar door, which stood half open.

"The noise is coming from downstairs," he said.

The twins got up and tiptoed to the basement door. The ticking sounded louder.

"What do you suppose it is?" Nan asked.

As the children listened Bert looked worried.

"Nan," he said, "why don't we go down and see if something's wrong?"

CHAPTER XIV

DANCING STICKS

"TURN on the light," Nan whispered.

Bert felt along the wall and found the switch. He flipped it and a dim light went on in the cellar below. They could see no one.

Cautiously the twins went down the stairs. The ticking sound grew louder. Nan pointed to a latticed door in one corner of the cellar.

"The noise is in there," she whispered.

The children walked across the earthen floor to the door. Bert quietly opened it. Once again he felt for a wall switch and flicked it. A ceiling light revealed a small work room. On a long table stood a big black metal box with a numbered dial on it. The clicking sound was coming from inside.

"It's some kind of an electric meter," Bert said.

Nan did not reply. Speechless, she pulled her

brother's sleeve and pointed to three hazel rods propped in the corner.

The sticks were twitching!

"But that's impossible!" Bert exclaimed.

"I can't believe it!" said Nan. "They're dancing all by themselves."

The Bobbseys took their eyes from the moving sticks and stared at the work table. Small shining parts were lying on top of it, helter-skelter. Here and there were bunches of different colored wires.

"It looks as if Mr. Finn is making something electrical," Bert remarked.

The next moment there were loud footsteps overhead, then the doodlebug's voice boomed out. "What are you doing down there? Spying on my secret?" He ran pellmell down the stairs. "I thought I told you to wait in the kitchen!" he cried, his face growing red.

"We did," said Bert, "but we heard a loud ticking down here and we were afraid something was wrong."

"Yes," Nan added. "We thought we ought to try to turn it off."

The doodlebug bit his lip and pushed past them. He flicked a switch on the meter and the ticking stopped.

"I forgot to turn this off," he muttered.

"What does it do?" Bert asked.

"Oh, it just measures some electricity I'm using," the dowser said.

Nan was eying the rods in the corner. They were still moving.

"Mr. Finn," she said, "please, won't you tell us what makes those sticks move?"

"No, I won't!" exclaimed the old man. "You have no business snooping down here!"

"We're very sorry," Bert said. "We thought we were helping."

As Bert looked around at the small parts on the table, the meter, and the twitching rods, he got an idea. "I'll bet I know your secret about the twitching sticks," he said. "You've invented an electronic doodlebug rod."

The elderly man stared at Bert. "How did you guess?" he whispered.

Bert gestured around the room. "It was easy. Nan and I just put two and two together."

With a sigh Mr. Finn sat down in the chair before the work bench. He buried his head in his hands. "Now my secret's out!"

"Oh, we won't tell," Nan assured him. Then she added quickly, "Would you care if we told our mother and the young twins?"

"No, of course not!" the old man said unhappily. "What I'm worried about is that everyone will find out and someone will steal my idea."

"None of us Bobbseys will tell, I promise you," said Nan firmly.

"How come you invented this, Mr. Finn?" Bert asked.

"At present the only people who can use a divining rod are the water witches like myself," Mr. Finn replied. "But with my electronic doodlebug anybody can find underground water. It'll be a great help to farmers and ranch owners and people who build houses out in the country —in fact, to anybody who needs a well."

"That sounds like a great idea," said Nan warmly. "How does it work?"

"I may as well tell you," the inventor said with a sigh. "I call my invention a water witch —WW for short." He picked up a tiny metal box from the table. "This is the electronic part that can locate water underground."

Then he took a miniature hammer and explained that the box was wired to it and both were put inside a hazel rod.

"When the box finds water it starts the hammer knocking and that's what makes the rods twitch."

"Then there must be water under the cellar," Nan said.

"Yes," the old man replied. "I found a stream under this floor some time ago. I use it to test my WWs. You'll notice that one of the rods is wired to this meter. I was measuring how long the battery would last."

"I'll bet I know your secret about the twitching sticks."

Nan told the dowser how she and Freddie had found the pile of sticks in the gully.

"Yes, I sneaked into the hazel grove to collect those," he replied. "I even went there at night, because I was afraid someone would see me and catch on to what I was doing."

Nan remarked that most of the sticks had been broken. "I guess it's hard to get the little boxes and hammers inside them."

The elderly man nodded sadly. "Yes, that's the hitch. I'm trying to find an easy way to insert the WW but so far I've had no luck."

Bert looked thoughtful. "Maybe you wouldn't have to put it in a real stick," said Bert. "Why don't you use plastic hazel wands with a hollow place in them for the WW?"

The old man's blue eyes widened. "I think you've got something there!" he exclaimed. "I have a friend in the plastic business. I'll write to him about it." He smiled. "Thanks a lot. I have to admit that's the best idea yet!"

"We have a surprise for you, Mr. Finn," said Nan as the inventor led them out of the workshop. "We found your binoculars in the ravine." She told him about the Bobbseys' adventure.

The old man looked pale as he listened. "I'm glad you escaped those fellows," he said. Then the doodlebug shook his head. "So *they* stole my binoculars."

"I'm sure that's what happened," said Bert.

"Where are the glasses?" the old man asked.

"On the kitchen table," said Nan.

The inventor turned out the light, shut the door and led the way up out of the cellar. The kitchen was dark, and he lit a lamp on the wall.

"Yes, these are my glasses all right," he said, picking up the binoculars. "Well, I guess I owe Robin Talltree an apology." He squared his shoulders. "We'll go now and I'll give it to her right away."

Twenty minutes later the doodlebug strode into the lobby of the Sky House with the older twins. It was crowded with the searchers who were listening to Officer Sanders.

"We want to thank everyone for helping," he said, "and especially the Bobbsey twins, who found Bleep."

As everyone applauded, the young twins smiled, and Bert and Nan blushed.

Mr. Finn cleared his throat. "I want to thank them, too." He explained how the twins had found his binoculars. "I apologize to you, Robin," said the old man, going over to the Indian girl. "I hope you will forgive me."

"Of course I will," she said quietly.

"First thing tomorrow," the doodlebug went on, "I'll go down to the playground and dowse for water."

Robin smiled happily. "That'll be wonderful, Mr. Finn!"

The guests applauded again. Then the crowd began to break up. After the police left, Mr. Finn invited the Bobbseys and Robin to his house for supper two nights later.

The twins and their Indian friend accepted, but Mrs. Bobbsey said she could not go. "I'm sorry," she explained. "I promised some of the ladies here I'd be in a skit with them that evening. But the twins can go without me."

As the doodlebug left for his home, Nan asked, "Where's Bleep?"

"The doctor came and taped his ankle," her mother replied, "and now he's resting." She added that everyone had eaten, but the dining room staff had kept food warm for Nan and Bert.

"And can I eat it!" said Bert. "I'm starved."

At the table the older twins told the rest of the family about Mr. Finn's invention. All promised to keep the secret.

When the Bobbseys came out of the dining room, they saw Mr. Moony and Mr. Hobbs pick up their keys at the desk and head for the elevator. As soon as the doors had closed behind the men, Bert and Nan went to the clerk and inquired if Miss Leaf was in her room.

"No. She's been out all day," the young man answered. "Mr. Hobbs and Mr. Moony were away, too," he added. "They all missed the excitement of the search."

"I'll bet they didn't miss anything," Nan remarked quietly as the twins walked away. "I think they were the three in the ravine!"

Bert agreed, and they walked over to the young twins, who were watching television with Mrs. Bobbsey.

Bert whispered to them, "Who wants to help with our Funny Wheels for the contest?"

"Oh, I do!" cried Flossie and Freddie. "Where?"

"The lifeguard Ken said we could work on it secretly in the beach house," Bert told them. "If you'll come with me now, I'll show you the secret plans."

Their mother accompanied the twins down the path and across the moonlit sand to the beach house. Bert opened the door and turned on the light. Next he took a piece of paper from his pocket and showed the others his drawing.

"It's a giant bug!" Nan exclaimed.

"A doodlebug!" cried Flossie.

"What can we make it out of?" Freddie asked.

"From all this junk," said Bert.

He swept his arm around the room. Scattered about were a door, part of an old canoe, two worn mattresses, four roller skates, a couple of boards and a frayed football. "This stuff was stored here. Ken said we could use it and also his tools."

"How'll we begin?" Flossie asked.

"First we nail two skates to each board. Then we attach the boards to the bottom with the skates showing. Next we nail the canoe to it upside down. We'll pack the mattress over that and cover the whole thing with canvas from an old sail. Then we paint it."

"What color?" Nan asked.

Bert grinned. "The rest of you decide."

Nan and the small twins thought their bug should look funny. Finally they chose a light blue body with dark blue spots. The head and feet were to be pink. The bug's antennae and tail would be red.

"He'll be bee-yoo-ti-ful!" cried Flossie.

Mrs. Bobbsey smiled. "It's a very original idea, Bert. Maybe it'll win a prize."

"What's the football for?" Freddie asked.

"The bug's head. We'll stick a big nail in the front end and tie the ball on there."

Bert took an old sail out of a box. Then he dragged a tool chest from a corner and the twins set to work eagerly. Gradually the high-domed back of the bug took shape.

As they were tacking the stiff canvas cover over the mattress, Freddie glanced up. The door to the beach house was slowly opening a crack!

"Someone's peeking!" Freddie whispered.

CHAPTER XV

FLOSSIE FLIES

AS THE other twins turned to look, the door to
the beach house quickly closed again.

"Somebody's spying on us!" Bert exclaimed.
"Let's see who it is!"

The twins dashed outside and saw a figure
racing across the moonlit sand toward the path.

"It's Danny!" Nan and Flossie cried out.

"Wouldn't you know it!" said Bert in disgust.

"I'll bet he's sorry he didn't build a Funny
Wheels," said Freddie.

The twins went back into the beach house and
finished tacking up the canvas.

"How are we going to make our doodlebug
run?" Nan asked as she tidied the place.

"It'll go by itself," Bert replied. "The course
is downhill. I wish we could lock this place but
there's no key."

"I doubt that anyone will bother your work

tonight," said Mrs. Bobbsey, "and tomorrow Ken will be here."

Early the next morning Robin drove the Bobbseys and the Ruggs to the playground lot in Red Feather to watch Mr. Finn locate water for a swimming pool.

"Look at all the people!" Freddie exclaimed. "The whole town is here!"

"I guess they are," said Robin. "Everybody's eager to watch Mr. Finn."

"What's that?" asked Freddie, pointing to a large piece of machinery standing at one side. It was a thin, towering framework with a heavy motor mounted on a truck.

"That's well-digging equipment," Bert replied. "The men are ready. They're just waiting for the doodlebug to tell them where to dig."

The Bobbseys threaded their way among the people to where Mr. Finn was standing. The elderly man held up his hands for silence and everyone became quiet.

From his back pocket he pulled a V-shaped rod of hazelwood. He held it up before his face and walked slowly across the lot. The crowd watched silently. Suddenly there was a light gasp and a murmur.

The rod was slowly coming downward!

"And Mr. Finn's hands aren't moving," Mrs. Bobbsey said quietly.

The rod dipped steadily until the tip of the V

pointed straight to the ground. The doodlebug stopped.

"This is the place," he announced.

The crowd cheered as the well-digging equipment was driven to the spot.

"The drilling will take awhile, folks," called one of the workmen. "The fire department will blow the siren when we strike water."

As the drill began to bore into the earth, the crowd broke up.

"Oh, that was wonderful, Mr. Doodlebug," Flossie cried as the old man walked over to them.

Robin beamed. "Thank you so much!"

Nan smiled and whispered, "Did the stick do it alone, or did you use your water witch?"

"Usually I do it myself," he told her quietly, "but this time I used my WW."

While the well-diggers worked, the hotel party went to the main street. The twins bought painting supplies for their Funny Wheels. Meanwhile Danny walked off by himself.

Robin and the two mothers went shopping. Later they all met at the Crystal Soda Shop. The group had just finished milk shakes when the fire siren blew loudly.

"Hooray!" cried Freddie. "They've struck water!"

"Now the playground can have a pool," said Nan.

"What about the swings and rides?" Flossie asked the Indian girl.

"They're coming from a big store on the highway," Robin replied. "The mayor and some of his friends are going down this afternoon to get them. Then everybody in town will help put them up, because we want to have the playground ready for Homecoming. That's day after tomorrow."

"We'd better hurry and get our Funny Wheels ready!" Freddie said.

"Forget it!" Danny sneered. "You'll never win with that crazy thing!"

"Maybe not, but we'll have a lot of fun," said Nan.

When the Bobbseys reached the hotel, the twins hurried to the beach house to work on their doodlebug. Bert opened the paint cans and laid out brushes while the others spread old newspapers on the floor. In a few minutes everyone was working.

By noontime Flossie had red paint on her nose and Freddie had two navy blue knees. But most of the colors were on the doodlebug.

"He looks wonderful," Nan said as they all stood back and admired the big bright bug.

Flossie beamed. "I'd just love to pat him on the head, he's so cute! But he's all wet."

After lunch the twins went looking for the Do-Re-Mees. In the Rec Room, they found Hal and Cal tuning their rented guitars. Bop was polishing his trumpet. Bleep sat on the edge of the platform.

"Hi!" he said. "How's your mystery coming?"

Bert shook his head. "We don't know anything new. But there's one good thing." He told about Mr. Finn finding water on the playground.

Bleep smiled. "Good ole doodlebug. I'm glad he came through!"

"Are you going to rehearse pretty soon?" Freddie asked eagerly. "And whatever you do with the ladder, will you do it now?"

"No," said Bleep sadly. "That's out for sure."

"What is the act?" Nan asked.

"Bleep dives off it," said Hal and Cal together.

"Dives?" the twins chorused.

"That's right," Bop said. "We play fast and loud with Bleep at the drums. Then he runs to the top of the ladder with the cymbals, clashes them together, spreads his arms, and flies off in a swan dive."

"Whoosh!" cried Bleep, spreading his arms.

Bop said, "Cal and Hal and I drop what we're doing and catch him in mid-air."

"Ooh, how 'citing!" Flossie exclaimed.

Hal went on, "Bleep picks up the tune on the drums, and crash, bang, BOOM BOOM BOOM, we hit the big finale!"

"It sounds cool!" Bert laughed.

"It is, man, it is," said Bleep. "But on account of my ankle the act is out."

"I'd do the flying act," said Hal, "but I'm too heavy."

"We're all too heavy," said Bop glumly.

"I'm not!" Flossie piped up. "And I'd love to go flying. Why don't you let me do it?"

Everyone looked surprised.

"You can't do that, Floss," said Nan. "I don't think the Do-Re-Mees want a little girl in their act."

The musicians exchanged looks. "Wait a minute there. That might not be a bad idea at all," said Bop.

A big smile spread over Bleep's face. "The more I think of it the better I like it! Where's your mother, Flossie?"

"On the porch," Bert put in, starting for the door. "I'll ask her."

The children and the musicians waited anxiously. A few moments later Bert came dashing back.

"It's okay, Floss! But Mother says you must do exactly as the Do-Re-Mees say."

Flossie clapped her hands. "Oh goody, goody!"

"You sit here next to me while I play the drums," said Bleep. He led Flossie onto the platform and gave her instructions.

At his signal Flossie took the cymbals and ran up the ladder. When she got to the very top the little girl stood up straight.

"That's it!" cried Bop. "Now bang the cymbals together, spread your arms wide and dive off."

"Like this, like this!" Freddie called and showed her how to swing her arms and hold her head.

Just at that moment Mrs. Bobbsey appeared at the back of the Rec Room. "Wait! Wait!" she cried. "I've changed my mind!"

"It's all right, Mommy!" Flossie called. "I'm not afraid." With that she clashed the cymbals together, spread her arms wide and dived off.

"Catch her!" cried Mrs. Bobbsey.

Instantly Hal and Cal reached up and caught the little girl neatly in mid-air. With a swing they set her on her feet and madly played the end of the number. The twins cheered and Mrs. Bobbsey smiled in relief.

"How was I, Mommy?" Flossie asked, rushing over to her mother.

Mrs. Bobbsey put both arms around her daughter. "You were great," she said.

"May she do it for the performance tonight, Mother?" Nan asked.

Mrs. Bobbsey nodded. "All right. After all, the men caught her safely." Flossie danced a jig of happiness.

"Now dive!" the musician said

"You'll need a costume of some kind," her mother remarked thoughtfully. "I'll make one this afternoon."

"Oh, thank you, Mrs. Bobbsey," said Bleep, and the other musicians joined him.

"I want to do it again!" cried Flossie and Freddie begged for a chance to fly off the ladder too.

"Okay," said Bleep. "Once for each of you. And remember," he added seriously, "this flying business is nothing to play around with. You must never try to do it unless a strong grownup is there to catch you." The young twins promised.

Afterward Nan and Bert stopped at the desk to see if Miss Leaf had returned.

"She's in," said the clerk, "but I'm afraid you can't see her. Miss Leaf came back late last night and left word she's not to be disturbed." He explained that the woman had said she was ill.

Disappointed, the older twins thanked the young man and turned away from the desk. They stayed around the hotel lobby hoping that Miss Leaf, Mr. Hobbs or Mr. Moony might appear. But none of them did.

That evening all the Bobbseys went to the Rec Room for the Do-Re-Mees' performance. Flossie's mother had made her a pair of red trousers and a short jacket like those the musicians wore.

At the right moment Bop said, "Dive!" and the little girl did her part perfectly. The audience applauded wildly, and the musicians presented her with a big bunch of flowers.

Afterwards Mrs. Bobbsey said, "I'm very proud of you, Flossie."

"Wait until you see our Funny Wheels in the contest!" Freddie spoke up. "Then you'll be proud of all of us."

His mother laughed and gave her small son a hug. "I'm proud of you twins all the time."

Bert suggested that they show the doodlebug on wheels to their mother right now.

"Let me put my bouquet in the water first," said Flossie, and skipped off.

Five minutes later she came back, and Bert led the way down the path and across the sand to the beach house. He opened the door and turned on the light.

"There it is!" Nan cried. "What do you—"

She stopped short. Everyone gasped in dismay.

The doodlebug was covered with wet black paint!

CHAPTER XVI

H—I—M

"OUR doodlebug is ruined!" exclaimed Nan.

The other twins and their mother stared unbelievingly. Bert stepped over to the giant canvas bug and touched his finger to the black paint. "It's still runny. This wasn't done long ago."

Freddie said, "I'll bet Danny did it!"

His mother shook her head. "I don't think so. Look! That's grownup printing," she said.

On the wall behind them someone had printed in black paint:

BOBBSEYS GO HOME!

"The gang again!" Bert exclaimed.

Flossie looked sad. "Our poor doodlebug! What can we do?"

Bert thought the best thing to do was let the black coating dry. "Then we'll paint our doodlebug over again."

The family returned to the hotel and Mrs.

Bobbsey reported the damage to the manager.

Nan and Bert decided to go back alone in the morning before breakfast to look for clues. The sun was just peeping over the treetops when they met and hurried down to the deserted waterfront. Bert lifted the latch of the beach house, and they slipped inside. The damaged doodlebug stood as they had left it.

Nan touched her finger lightly to the black paint. "It's dry."

"Good. We can fix it up this morning," said Bert.

The twins looked around the room for a clue to the person who had dumped the paint over their Funny Wheels.

"Here's a clue!" Nan exclaimed. On the white wall was a large black thumb print.

Bert gave a low whistle. "That's the biggest one I've ever seen."

"It might be Mr. Moony's," Nan remarked. "He's a very big man."

At breakfast she and Bert told the rest of the family where they had been.

As they finished Robin came over to the Bobbseys' table. "This is my day off," she said. "Would you twins like to go to the playground with me after lunch and help put up the new equipment?"

"We'd love to," said Nan and the others.

When the children told her about their doodlebug, Robin looked troubled. "You must be getting very warm on the mystery," she said, "because whoever is doing all this mischief certainly wants to get rid of you."

The four twins hastened to the beach house. Ken was standing nearby, and said Mr. Voss had told him to put a lock on the door.

Just then they heard a loud yell. "Watch out, everybody! Here I come!" They all turned to see Danny seated in an old rowboat on wheels. It did not move.

Bert grinned. "You're not going any place, Danny!"

"I know it!" called the boy. "I was just testing." He climbed out of the boat and began pounding on the wheels.

The lifeguard shook his head. "I let him have that old rowboat and some coaster-wagon wheels that we had around here. I'm afraid he put it together too fast."

Bert grinned. "I thought he'd change his mind about going in the contest."

The twins hurried into the beach house and started brushing light blue paint over the black canvas. In an hour the doodlebug was restored.

"Now he needs reins so I can steer him," said Bert.

"Why can't we all ride?" Freddie asked.

"Okay," his brother agreed. He attached ropes to the ends of the front skate board.

"How about stirrups for our feet?" Nan suggested. "Otherwise we'll fall off."

"Good idea," said her twin. Bert tacked four canvas loops to each side of the bug.

"Our bug is all ready to go!" exclaimed Nan.

The door was locked, and the children went back to Sky House. Bert and Nan hurried to the desk and inquired again about Miss Leaf.

"You just missed her," the clerk said. "She went out for the day."

"How about Mr. Hobbs and Mr. Moony?" Nan asked.

The clerk checked the mail boxes to see if the room keys were there. "The men are out, too."

The children changed into fresh clothes for lunch. Immediately after eating, they started for the parking lot to meet Robin. On the way they saw Bleep, and Bert told him about the note in the beach house.

"That gang is still around, all right," the musician said. "You'd better be careful."

"How about you?" Nan asked. "If they think you can identify them, they'll try to kidnap you again."

Bleep shook his head. "They know that if I could have, I'd have done it right away. I don't think they'll bother with me now."

During the conversation Flossie had run ahead to the parking lot. When the others came up, she was standing beside a man poking under the hood of his automobile. She was holding her little cardboard bug box in one hand.

"What are you doing, Floss?" Nan asked.

"This man said there's a bug in his car," said Flossie. "I'm waiting for it to come out."

The man wiped his face wearily and grinned. "It's not that kind of a bug, little girl." The other children laughed. "He means there's something wrong with the motor," Bert explained.

"Oh," said Flossie, her face turning pink. "I thought maybe it was a doodlebug and I could catch him in my box."

She slipped the box into her pocket and followed the other children to the station wagon. Robin arrived a few moments later, and they set off for town.

On the way Nan's thoughts turned to the sidewalk message about the Calico Cat. She took a pencil and pad from her purse and jotted it down. "Meet him in Calico Cat," she read aloud. "But who is *him?*"

"Maybe it was the pet store man," Freddie suggested.

Thoughtfully Nan wrote the names Hobbs, Ivy, and Moony. Then she added fancy squiggles to the words.

Flossie looked over her shoulder. "You're doodling."

"I know. I'm trying to get an idea." Suddenly she gave a little gasp. "Oh! Why didn't I think of this before?"

"What do you mean?" Bert asked.

"H-I-M!" Nan exclaimed. "Those letters could stand for *H*obbs, *I*vy and *M*oony. Maybe HIM is a code name for the three of them, and the message meant they should all meet at Calico."

"That's smart, Nan," said Bert.

Robin agreed. "Of course it's not proof that Hobbs, Ivy and Moony are gang members," she reminded the twins, "but it certainly makes it look that way. Well, here we are."

Robin parked on the street by the playground. On one side of it men were busy erecting a long stand of swings. A red-haired boy was watching them.

"Look!" said Freddie. "There's the boy who stopped our car!"

"Let's question him," said Bert. But when the twins hurried forward, the freckle-faced lad turned and ran into the woods behind the playground.

"Stop!" called Bert. "We want to talk to you!"

As the boy ran faster, Bert sprinted ahead and brought him down with a flying tackle.

"Ow! Let me up!" the boy cried.

Bert let him sit up. "What was the big idea of

telling us there was an injured man in the woods?" he asked.

The redhead looked at the twins and Robin, who had surrounded him.

"I didn't mean any harm," he said. "Some big guy came up to me in front of the candy store and asked if I wanted to earn some money. All I had to do was play a joke on some friends of his."

"What did this man look like?" Robin questioned.

As the boy described the man, the listeners exchanged glances. It sounded like Mr. Moony!

"Okay, you can go now," said Bert, "but I wouldn't play any more bad jokes like that. You could get into trouble."

Without a word the boy jumped up and ran.

"Everything points to Moony and Hobbs," Bert remarked.

After helping some of the townspeople put up climbing bars and seesaws, the twins returned to the hotel with Robin.

"Don't forget our date at Mr. Finn's house for dinner," she reminded them.

"We'll be ready," Nan promised.

The sun was going down when Bert and Nan rowed the young twins across the lake to the doodlebug's dock. A few minutes later Robin paddled up in her canoe. Mr. Finn came down to meet them.

"Stop!" cried Bert

"We have steak and french fries and all the trimmings," the dowser said, as he led them straight to a round table in the kitchen. It was set with pretty blue china on a red-checked cloth. "I even made apple pie," he added, taking two large tins from the oven.

"Everything was yummy, Mr. Doodlebug," said Flossie when they finished.

"Coming over here tonight," Robin spoke up, "reminded me of how I used to play in the lookout when I was a child. My friends and I signaled each other from there with flashlights."

"That sounds like fun," said Freddie. "What messages did you send?"

"Our favorite was, 'Come quickly and bring many braves.'" Robin smiled. "The children who were supposed to be the rescue party usually waited across the lake. Their leader would reply, 'We're on our way.'"

"Do you remember how the signals went?" Bert asked curiously.

"Of course I do," said Robin, chuckling. "I stood in the lookout window and made five big crisscrosses in the air with my flashlight."

"And what was the answering signal?" Flossie put in.

"Two big crisscrosses in the air," Robin replied.

After talking a little longer, Robin glanced at her watch. "I must go now," she said, and thanked Mr. Finn for a lovely dinner.

The twins were happy to see her and the old man shake hands on the front porch. The Indian girl hurried to the dock and paddled away in the moonlight.

The twins stayed a little longer, then stood up to go. The doodlebug saw them to the door.

After the children had thanked him, he smiled and said, "It's I who should thank you. You gave me a wonderful idea for my doodlebug. I called my friend who makes plastics, and he said that it would be easy to manufacture rods with the WW inside."

The children congratulated him and said good night.

"I'll see you again soon," the old man promised. He yawned. "Right now I'm going straight to bed."

Using their flashlights, the twins walked down the path to the dock. As they were about to step into their boat, they glanced back and saw the lights go out in Mr. Finn's house.

Bert chuckled. "He really did go right to bed."

The next moment Bert gasped and pointed up to the lookout. A flare was waving in a big circle.

"The lookout spooks!" quavered Flossie.

"That's right," said Bert in a low, excited voice. "And I'll bet they're Moony, Hobbs, and Ivy. Now's our chance to find out!"

CHAPTER XVII

THE TWANGING MOUSE

"TURN out your flashlights—quick!" said Nan. "We don't want whoever's in the lookout to see us."

The other twins obeyed and dashed off the dock into the shadow of some trees.

Bert glanced up at the torch, which was still waving in the window. "We'd better hurry," he said, "if we want to find out who's signaling."

Swiftly and quietly the children went through Mr. Finn's back yard, crossed the gully and went up the hill. At the top they slipped into the lookout. It was pitch-black.

Holding hands, the twins edged around the wall until Bert came to the first step of the stone stairway. He moved quietly up four steps, and the other children each stood on one behind him.

Suddenly a deep voice came from the upper room. "Stop waving that torch, Ivy. The fellows must have seen it by now."

"I hope so, Hobbs," replied a high, thin voice.

"I don't see why we have to do this," Hobbs complained. "You telephoned them about the meeting."

"I've explained it to you a hundred times," said Ivy crossly. "The torch means the coast is clear and it's safe to carry out the plans."

"We're wasting time staying here," said a third voice. "The cops checked on the pet store, and there's no telling when they'll catch up with us."

"They're not going to get us, Moony," said Ivy coldly.

The twins squeezed one another's hands in excitement. They were right about the three men!

"If you ask me, those Bobbsey twins tipped off the police about Calico," Moony went on.

"What about the cat store guy?" asked Hobbs. "How's he going to get here?"

"A couple of the other fellows will pick him up in Red Feather."

"It was a good idea using the pet shop for our number-two hideout," Ivy added. "I took one look at that fellow and knew he'd be useful."

"Bristol's okay, boss," grumbled Moony, "but you took a chance bringing him into the gang. And stealing those guitars was risky. You're taking too many chances, Ivy."

"I'm the boss," said Ivy coldly.

"We should have got out of here long ago," Hobbs went on.

"We're staying until we pull the big job," said Ivy icily. "Those Bobbsey kids interrupted us once, but this time I'm going to get every cent in that safe."

"Stop arguing, Hobbs," put in Moony. "The boss just signaled the fellows to go to the number-one hideout and bring their loot. We'll make the final division tonight, and then everybody can clear out."

Ivy chuckled. "Everybody but us! We'll pull the Sky House job before we go. That way we won't have to split the money with the other fellows. What they don't know won't hurt 'em."

The other two laughed. "You fixed this lookout setup pretty cool, boss," Moony said.

"Until you nearly spoiled it," said Ivy. "When you stole the binoculars and the bird book, the old doodlebug accused the Indian girl. That stirred up the Bobbsey twins."

"Was that my fault?" retorted Moony. "I figured if I stole that stuff the old dowser wouldn't be using this place to watch birds."

"And another thing, Ivy," said Hobbs. "It was your stupid idea to put the message on the sidewalk in Red Feather. Those Bobbseys saw it and headed straight for Calico the next day."

"What else could we do?" Moony asked.

"You two were out of the hotel all day, and so was I. How could we get in touch?"

For a while the three men were silent. Then Hobbs spoke up again. "It'll take an hour for the fellows to get here. We've had too many close calls. I still shake when I think of that day the twins came to Calico!"

"Yes," said Moony, "you should have stayed in the back of the shop, Ivy, until the twins were gone."

"I didn't know they were there," he replied sharply. "When I came out the place was full of cats and kids. It was too late to go back."

"Lucky we weren't in the store, too," said Hobbs. "They'd have seen us all together."

"They almost did," said Moony. "We had to get to Red Feather fast."

"Yes," said Hobbs, "and that's where we heard about the big search for Bleep."

"Don't I know it!" exclaimed Moony. "We took the Calico loot to the number-one hideout and then went back to the ravine to check on the musician, and found him gone."

"We're mighty lucky Bleep didn't recognize our voices and blab," muttered Hobbs.

While the twins listened, Flossie's foot went to sleep. Shifting her position, she hit a loose pebble which rattled down the steps.

"What was that?" Ivy asked sharply.

"I'll go see," Moony offered.

The twins froze in alarm. Suddenly Bert had an idea. He began to bark like a dog.

"Never mind," said Ivy. "It's just a dog."

With sighs of relief the children crept down the steps and out of the lookout.

"We must alert the police," said Bert.

"We could row over to the Sky House," Nan suggested, "and phone from there. Only we don't know where hideout number one is. By the time they get here the men would probably be gone."

Bert agreed. "I can't help thinking that the houseboat has something to do with the gang. It may be hideout number one."

"I believe you're right," said Nan. "Remember that funny twanging noise on the houseboat? It could have come from a guitar. If the stolen guitars are there, that proves the houseboat is the hideout!"

The children were excited by the idea. "Let's go see!" said Freddie.

The twins made their way down the hill in darkness. At the bottom they decided it was safe to turn on their flashlights. They kept the beams trained on the ground all the way to the houseboat.

"Freddie and I'll go aboard and take a look," Bert whispered. "Nan, you and Flossie keep watch."

The two boys crossed the narrow beach and

stepped onto the deck. The boards creaked as they walked to the door. Bert put his hand cautiously on the handle and turned it. To his surprise the door was unlocked. He pushed it open and shone his light into the darkness.

In the moving beam the brothers saw rickety old furniture. The two guitars were propped in one corner.

"Nan was right!" Freddie whispered. "This is the hideout, after all!"

"Let's take a quick look around," said Bert. "Then we'll run and tell Mr. Finn. He can go across the lake in his motorboat and call the police from the Sky House."

Across the room from the guitars Bert spotted a cat-carrier. "I'll bet it's the box we saw Ivy taking from the pet store."

He laid his light on the floor, then lifted the two latches on the sides of the carrier and raised the lid.

"Wow! Money!" Freddie exclaimed. The black box was full of neat packages of greenbacks.

"This must be the loot from the Calico robbery," Bert remarked as he closed the lid again.

"Here's Mr. Doodlebug's bird book!" Freddie cried as he turned his light on a nearby chair.

Bert opened the book. On the fly leaf was the name *F. C. Finn*. Next to the chair was a large canvas bag. Freddie opened it and looked in.

"This is the hideout," Freddie whispered

"More money!" he exclaimed. The boys took out several packages of bills. One was labeled *Game Farm*. The others had the names of neighboring hotels on them.

"Where do you suppose all this stuff was when the police checked this place?" Freddie asked as the boys put the money back in the bag.

The older boy shrugged. "The gang must have hidden the stuff somewhere else until the search was over."

"Maybe in the ravine," Freddie suggested, " 'cause that's where we found the binoculars."

His brother nodded. "Very likely."

Suddenly there came a loud *TWANG* from behind them. The boys whirled toward the guitars. Bert turned his light on the instruments, just in time to catch a small furry body scurrying across the strings.

"A mouse!" Bert exclaimed. "That explains the spooky twanging noise we heard the day we found Bleep. We'd better get out of here and call the police."

When the boys stepped onto the deck, they were suddenly bathed in the fierce glare of a powerful flashlight.

"Those twins again!" boomed Moony. "Catch them!"

Before the boys could move, strong arms had seized them both.

CHAPTER XVIII

THE TWINS' BIG JOB

"HELP!" yelled Freddie.

The next moment a large hand was clapped over his mouth and another over Bert's. The boys were hustled back into the houseboat.

One of the men took away the boys' flashlights and lit an oil lamp on the table. In the dim glow Bert and Freddie saw three men.

"You kids sit against the wall over there and keep quiet," Ivy ordered angrily.

"And no tricks," rumbled Moony.

"What are we going to do with them?" Hobbs asked.

"We'll take care of 'em after the meeting," said Ivy in his high, unpleasant voice.

Moony gave a short laugh. "They've made plenty of trouble for us. And my dear Miss Leaf," he added sarcastically, "your attempt to wreck the Bobbseys' kite boat didn't get them off our necks, now did it?"

"The main trouble," said Ivy nastily, "is that some idiot forgot to lock the door of this houseboat. Who was that?"

"I forgot. So what?" Hobbs replied angrily. "We should have left the loot in the ravine the first time we moved it there. Now these kids have seen it."

"Never mind. They're through making mischief," said Ivy. He glared at the boys. "Where are your sisters?"

"I don't know," Bert replied honestly.

At that moment the two frightened girls were racing through the woods toward the lookout. Nan had decided to give Robin's childhood signal. "Maybe Robin will see it and send help."

By the time the girls reached the hilltop, Flossie's chubby legs were aching. But she clung to Nan's hand and climbed the steps. From the window they could see the lights of the hotel and Robin's cottage.

Nan swung her flashlight in big crisscrosses the way the Indian girl had described.

"Oh, I hope she sees it," Flossie said.

Nan finished the signal and waited. There was no answering light on the far shore. Once again she swept the beam through the air.

"She saw it!" Nan exclaimed as two answering crisscrosses appeared across the lake. "Now she'll get the police—unless she thinks we're just playing a game."

"But meantime the bad men have Bert and Freddie," said Flossie, tears running down her cheeks.

"Let's get Mr. Finn to help," Nan said.

The girls hurried down the hill, crossed the gully, and dashed to the doodlebug's back door. They knocked loudly.

"Mr. Doodlebug!" Flossie called. "Wake up! Hurry! Help us!"

A light went on inside. A few minutes later Mr. Finn opened the door. He was wearing a red bathrobe and his white hair stood up in wisps all over his head.

"What's the matter?" he asked, alarmed.

Breathlessly Nan told the story. "The thieves came so quietly we didn't hear them. We had no chance to warn Bert and Freddie."

"Good gracious!" the old man exclaimed.

He dashed back into the house calling, "Wait there. I'll be right with you!" A few minutes later he hurried out, fully dressed.

"Listen, girls," the doodlebug said, "you wait at the dock and send the police to the cove. I'll go and try to free the boys."

Meanwhile, on the houseboat, the thieves paid no attention to Bert and Freddie, who were sitting quietly in the shadows.

Bert noticed that the wide, vertical board he was leaning against could be pushed out a little.

Not daring to speak, he took Freddie's hand and guided it to the board.

The little boy understood at once. He moved closer and helped push the plank outward. Soon they could lift it up far enough to crawl out. But at that moment heavy footsteps sounded on the deck.

"Here they come!" exclaimed Hobbs. He opened the door. Seven men stomped into the room.

"Okay, Ivy," the tallest one said. He tossed a canvas bag on the table. "There's the loot we got today. Now you bring out the money from the Game Farm, the movies, the hotels, and the Calico job."

Just then the pet store man spied the boys. "Those kids!" he exclaimed. "What are they doing here?"

The brothers' hearts sank as the others turned to look. It was too late to sneak out!

"They were snooping," said Moony.

"Never mind them," one of the newcomers cut in. "Let's divide the money."

"Don't worry, men," said Ivy smoothly. "We'll all get an equal share right now."

Suddenly Bert had an idea. "That's not what you said before, Mr. Ivy," he called loudly.

"You shut up," snapped the thief.

"Wait a minute!" said the tall man. "What's he talking about?"

"Mr. Doodlebug! Wake up! Help us!"
Flossie begged

"Hobbs, Ivy, and Moony are going to rob the Sky House tonight after you've gone," Bert said. "That'll be the biggest haul of all, and they won't have to share it with you."

There was a growl of anger among the men.

"Hold on! We can explain!" cried Ivy, but the men talked loudly and angrier.

Bert squeezed Freddie's arm. "Now!" he said. "Come on!"

While the thieves argued bitterly, the two boys lifted the loose board and crawled onto the deck. Swiftly they tiptoed ashore.

Psst! A hissing sound came from the woods. A white-haired figure stepped onto the beach.

"Mr. Doodlebug!" Freddie exclaimed. The brothers ran over to him, and they all slipped back among the trees. Quickly the three exchanged stories.

"We'd better get to my house," said Mr. Finn. "The police will be arriving soon."

"Wait a minute!" said Bert. "Suppose the thieves take the loot and go before the police can get here?"

"We can't let them escape now!" Freddie put in.

Mr. Finn frowned. "But what are we going to do? We're outnumbered."

"If there was only some way we could keep them bottled up on the houseboat," said Bert.

For a moment the three stood thinking. Then Bert snapped his fingers. "I know! We'll set them adrift!"

"Good idea!" said the doodlebug.

Bert looked around and spotted a stout oak branch on the ground. Quietly the three carried it onto the beach. The sound of shouting and crashing furniture came from the houseboat.

Bert placed one end of the limb against the side of the old craft. Then the two boys and the doodlebug pushed hard. The houseboat lifted slightly, then drifted clear of the sand. The trio gave it another strong shove, and it floated toward the mouth of the cove.

Freddie giggled. "The men are so busy fighting they don't know the boat's carrying them away!"

"It won't be long before that old tub will be out in the middle of the lake," said Mr. Finn with a chuckle.

He and the twins hurried to the doodlebug's dock. By this time the houseboat was drifting on the lake.

Moments later two big motorboats roared up to the dock. Officer Sanders climbed out of the first one and heard the news.

"Good work, children!" he said. "We'll round up those thieves and meet you at the Sky House dock."

Twenty minutes later a crowd of hotel people watched as the police marched the prisoners ashore.

Ivy scowled at the twins. "If it hadn't been for you, we'd have pulled off the big job tonight!"

"I'd say," Bleep called loudly, "it's the Bobbsey twins who pulled off the big job tonight!"

As everyone nodded, the officers herded the crestfallen gang into three squad cars and drove off.

The next morning Robin made a speech at the playground, giving it to the children of Red Feather. But Flossie was not listening with the rest of her family. Afterward Nan saw her stooping beside the shiny new swings, looking at the ground.

"I found a doodlebug!" Flossie called.

The other twins went over and she pointed to a small funnel-shaped pit. "Doodlebug, doodlebug, come out and play!" she begged.

The next moment a little spray of sand shot up out of the pit.

"She's right! It *is* a doodlebug!" said Bert.

Flossie clapped her hands. "I knew I'd find one! But I don't have my bug box!"

"That's all right," said Nan. "It'll be nicer for him to live here at the playground."

Just then Robin called out, "Hurry up! It's time for the Funny Wheels race."

The twins ran to join the crowd which was

moving to the slope outside of town. At the bottom the Do-Re-Mees were playing a gay tune, using their own guitars. At the top was the mayor with a microphone. Behind him Mr. Voss and Mr. Finn unloaded the Bobbseys' doodlebug and Danny's rowboat-on-wheels from the hotel pickup truck. A number of odd cars were lined along the road, ready to go.

Danny was first. *Clickety-clickety!* went his uneven wheels. The next moment one of them broke free. Spectators gasped as the rowboat swerved into a ditch.

"Are you hurt, son?" called the mayor.

"No, I'm not!" Danny yelled back. "But there's something wrong with the race track!"

Next the Bobbseys stood up on the back of their bug. Bert was in front with Flossie behind him holding onto his waist. Next was Nan, who held onto Flossie, then Freddie who grasped Nan's waist. As they put their feet in the stirrups, Bert took hold of the reins.

"Hang on!" Mrs. Bobbsey cried, and Robin gave the bug a push.

"Oh, it's fun!" cried Flossie as the Funny Wheels rolled down the slope past the laughing crowd.

At the end of the race the mayor announced that a bicycle with an umbrella over it had been the fastest vehicle.

"The funniest was the doodlebug," he announced. Each twin received a toy racing car as a prize.

Mr. Voss came over to congratulate them. "I'm afraid I misjudged you children," he said, "and I want to apologize. You see, I had heard a lot of very bad things about you."

As the twins looked puzzled, Danny pulled on Mr. Voss's sleeve. "Uncle Carl," he whined, "the race wasn't fair!"

The Bobbseys grinned. So Mr. Voss was Danny's uncle! No wonder he had heard bad things about them!

The manager turned to his nephew. "The twins won fair and square," he said sternly. "And I don't want to hear another word out of you!"

At that point Bleep called for quiet and the crowd stopped talking. "By now you have all heard how the Bobbsey twins caught the gang of thieves!" he said. "In honor of these great detectives we have changed the name of our group. From now on, we're going to be called the Doodlebugs!"